A FAMILY THAT SLAYS TOGETHER

Mama's Brood #3

SHAY RUCKER

WARNING:

This book contains sexually explicit scenes, graphic violence, themes of abuse, and adult language and content.

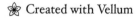 Created with Vellum

To Ma and Da. You have held it down and supported me in so many ways. Your continued love, cheerleading, dragggging about getting the writing done... All I can say is my spirit knew it was time to land when it found you. Love you guys.

CHAPTER ONE

How was she going to do this?

How was she going to walk into that beautiful home – with its champagne exterior and cranberry trim, garden with flowers in full bloom, porch with rocking chairs, swinging bench, and kid's bike – and take her niece away?

She'd *dreamed* of homes like this when she was Briana's age. Safe homes, homes with people who only wanted the best for you, were willing to make sacrifices for you instead of just sacrificing you.

She couldn't possibly give Briana all that the Jaces' had given her; she didn't know the first thing about parenting. And she wasn't a patient person, and her moral compass had never pointed in the direction of right with any regularity.

*Oh God, oh God, oh God...*What the hell was she doing here? She would ruin this kid.

Zeus banged on the passenger door.

She jumped, but kept her head pressed against her knees,

curled in fetal position as much as the passenger seat would allow.

There was a much more restrained tap against the window, and Sabrina lifted her head just enough to turn it to the right and see that familiar fitted dark gray t-shirt overlapping the waistband of Zeus's black jeans. Damn.

Sitting up, Sabrina rolled down the window midway.

On the other side of the pane, Zeus's fingers did a choreographed dance. She called this particular sequence the woman's-testing-my-patience dance.

Her facial muscles relaxed into a soft smile. He was keeping to their bargain; no blades within visibility of the Jace's; no actions to scare them away from relinquishing Briana to their care.

She began trembling internally again.

Despite her unconditional love for the little girl inside the house across the street, she was having misgivings, when Zeus – a man more comfortable with wildlife than people – had none.

Placing his arms on the roof of the car, Zeus bent down and held her gaze, silently communicating his impatience that she was wasting time trying to corral her foolish 'woman's brain chatter', when she should be outside standing beside him.

She wanted his clarity of purpose, his uncompromising certainty that this was the right thing to do.

"What if she sees me, like *really* sees me, Zeus – the way that only kids can – then decides she doesn't want to be with us? What if she decides I'm not good enough? What if she blames me for Samantha's death?" Her heart raced. "Why the fuck did you let me believe I could parent a kid?! All I've ever done remotely well was know when to get the hell out when things got too bad."

His gaze never drifted.

She wanted to punch him. She needed to do something besides hold on to this paralyzing fear.

"Say the word, I get back in the car and we drive away," Zeus said.

"Are you crazy? That's my niece in there, my only living relative; I can't just walk away from her!"

He cocked his brow, turned to look down the street for a moment before straightening. "Get out of the car."

Sabrina looked through the windshield, gazing at the tree lined street. It was fucking picturesque. Her presence felt like a blemish on something so wholesome.

She gritted her teeth and begrudgingly reached for the door, stepping out of the car, and slamming the door.

"You need a hug?" Zeus asked, when she stood in front of him.

Her shoulders fell and she nodded. Taking a step closer, she placed her forehead on his chest and his arms wound around her waist. His steady heart beat grounded her, but the fear was still there, telling her that she would ruin her niece's life, that Bri would be better off without her.

Yet that selfish need for connection, which metastasized the longer she was with Zeus and the Brood, urged her to do this.

"Can't move forward by running in place," Zeus said. "If you need holding, I'll hold you, but there's nothing more for us here. Inside the house is our future. Good and bad, plea-sure and pain. Standing here, we can't build our family, or stab people who need stabbing." He butted her head, forcing her to look up at him. "You know I gotta stab people, right?"

She laughed, tears falling as she circled her arms around his neck, and he lifted her off her feet.

"It's terrifying to love you this much," she whispered. "The idea of life without you literally terrifies me. The idea that you could be hurt leaves me sick. The idea that I can hurt you sometimes is agonizing, and I feel all of that for the little girl inside that perfect house, and I haven't even touched her yet Zeus. All this love...it's terrifying."

He set her back on her feet and stepped away, his face a neutral mask with penetrating silver-grey eyes.

Was this the moment? The one where he decided he'd finally filled his need of her and walk away, returning to his solitary existence?

"I wasn't sure before," Zeus said. "But I understand now."

And he just left her there, walked away, crossing the street as he moved towards the house, forcing her to jog to catch up.

As she approached the porch, he knocked on the door.

"What do you understand now?" She hissed, facing the door beside him, waiting for it to open, heart in her throat.

"What love is. It's connection... blade deep through the heart, but you bleed out willingly. And the feeling you get, you'd happily die for. It's unnatural. I understand why it terrifies you. It's not safe to love the wrong people, only the ones who love you the same way."

That was so freaking... unbelievably Zeus, she thought, staring at him at a loss for words.

After all their time together, *this* was when he realized he loves her? While she was in the middle of a freaking emotional breakdown; on the doorstep to a whole new life?

The lock on the other side of the door disengaged.

"Moving forward," Zeus muttered, as the door swung open.

Sabrina stared down at the wide-eyed, fairer-complexioned child; long thick hair tamed into two tight-against-the-scalp ponytails that promised chaos when set free. She wore a peach dress sporting a wide purple waist ribbon with a bow at the hip and matching purple patent leather shoes. This young Samora female was more stylishly dressed than Sabrina had ever been.

"Moving forward," Sabrina said as she kneeled, her heart thumping so hard she feared it was going to explode.

"You guys were out there forever," Bri said. "I watched you from the window and thought you were going to leave without me."

"I was scared," Sabrina replied honestly, reaching out to hold onto Briana's small hand. "I was afraid that you might not like me, or that you wouldn't want to leave your beautiful home."

"I was scared too." Briana said, looking down at their joined hands. "My mom never came. In the letters she promised me she would, but she never came."

Sabrina's heart broke all over again, thinking about the death of her sister. But the grief over how and why Sam died seemed to hit her every other day, instead of every other hour. It never left her, but its impact lessened as time passed.

Silent tears slid down Briana's face and for a moment Sabrina didn't know what to do, what to say. She couldn't stop the tears falling from her own eyes, an emotional wreck, and her niece needed her.

Pulling Briana into her arms, they cried, mourning Samantha and holding on to each other, holding on to hope for the future and holding on to love. As Bri quieted, Sabrina pulled back, wiping away both their tears.

"My sister loved you more than she loved anything in this

world, she only ever wanted you to be happy and loved and safe. That much I know."

Standing, Sabrina noticed Mrs. Jace in the foyer, her hand covered her mouth as tears ran down her face.

"Thank you," Sabrina mouthed, looking down when Zeus took a knee and pinned Briana with his mercurial gaze. They stared at each other as if their silence was its own form of communication.

"Do you feel stronger now?" Zeus asked eventually.

Briana nodded, wiping any residual moisture from her face.

"No chatter," she told Zeus, and Sabrina believed they were referring to one of his many lessons. One that Briana obviously passed.

"You're mine now," Zeus told Bri. "The Blade Spirits say it's so."

"No, you're *mine*, which means we're each other's." Briana said, teaching Zeus her own very important life lesson.

Zeus glared up at Sabrina as if she were somehow responsible for Briana voicing her perspective.

"Hey, that's not on me," Sabrina said holding up her hands. "That's my mother's genetic signature through and through."

Zeus picked Briana up and walked into the house with her on his hip, as if she were a two-year-old instead of a seven-soon-to-be-eight year old. He stopped in front of Mrs. Jace. "It's definitely her." He nodded back towards Sabrina.

"Well then son, with two strong young women, you better keep your wits about you," Mrs. Jace smiled.

Zeus grunted, dismissing Mrs. Jace's words as he mumbled something to Briana.

She pointed down the hallway towards an open entryway

on the left. Based on the enticing smells coming from that direction, Sabrina knew it was the kitchen.

"How long has it been since he's eaten?" Mrs. Jace asked, hugging Sabrina in greeting.

"Not since we left Mama's this morning. He's particular about where his food comes from."

"I don't envy the challenge you're about to have on your hands. Between the two of them, they're going to try and run you ragged. They'll try to double team you too. Him with logic, and her with those doe eyes." Mrs. Jace's eyes began to well again as she worried the edge of her cream, short-sleeved blouse. "Don't let them."

"How's Mr. Jace?"

"You know that child has known a lot of loss to be so young," Mrs. Jace said, not directly answering the question. "She's said her goodbyes to my husband, and when you all leave tomorrow she knows it'll be the last time she sees him alive. I think he held on this long just to make sure she would be okay."

"And you?" Sabrina asked. Folks sometimes forgot to ask this of women who stayed strong, holding down everyone and everything else. "How are *you* doing?"

Mrs. Jace kept her head down, shaking it side to side, tears silently falling. She pulled the older woman in her arms and held her as a damn of grief broke.

Mrs. Jace would lose her husband of over forty-five years when she took him off life support in a couple of days, and tomorrow she'd hand over the care of Briana, the child she'd raised since Bri was one day old.

Samantha had entrusted the Jaces, literal strangers, with Bri's care because back then Sabrina wasn't making choices that took into account even her own safety. If she'd just gotten it together sooner, she kept telling herself, she could've been there, could've helped Sam, could've stopped her from taking her own life after surviving hell.

"I'll be alright baby," Mrs. Jase said, pulling away and resetting her composure. "I'll be alright."

"We'll be in Europe for only a few weeks, and when we get back to the Bay Area, we'll be moving into the new house. Me, against Bri and Zeus, it'll be a challenge. But me and *you*.... All I'm saying is there's a reason Zeus bought a home with an in-law unit. I know it's a lot to uproot yourself after all these years, but if you ever want to, you have another home waiting for you."

"I had questions about you all in the beginning. Especially that man of yours. He's a whole lot of different, but all these weeks of face-timing, I know he cares about our little girl."

"He'd give up his life to protect hers," Sabrina said. She knew this because less than two months ago he'd been willing to do the same for her.

"That's how it should be. Kids these days need to be protected more than ever," Mrs. Jace said, smoothing her hands over her hips. "Now, let's get in the kitchen before those two get into my pots. I'm not above smacking a grown man for getting in my pots."

"And that's how it should be," Sabrina smiled, relishing in the look on Zeus's face if Mrs. Jace did.

He stood, partially hidden by the mature Red Maple tree, and gazed at the house across the street. The interior lights had gone out hours ago, the people inside slept. The love and laughter that had escaped through the open windows and screened front doors earlier, wouldn't shield them from what was to come.

Moving from behind the tree, he maneuvered through the seams of the moonless night as an ambassador of death, its emissary, and entered the home via the plant-filled sunroom. Passing the two rocking chairs with coffee table placed between, he paused, listened to the night, heard nothing of interest except the way death whispered as it moved through the house's interior.

Opening the door, he slipped inside and locked it behind him, pocketing the key. Nothing would get in or out now. They were all locked into this fate together.

Roaming downstairs, he felt death move in lockstep behind him, so close he wondered if there was any true distinction between it and him as he entered the older woman's room. He scented lilac and lavender, soft scents for a strong woman biding her time, until the real pain was upon her.

He pulled his knife, pressed the tip against the hollow of her throat, moved in close, so close he could still smell the antiseptic mint of mouthwash on her breath, the smoky black castor oil in hair bound by an old gray scarf. His cheek nearly touched hers as he listened in on the sadness of her dreams, as she whispered, then groaned. He turned the blade and pressed the flat of it against her collarbone.

She quieted.

So much pain on the way, its scouts already here.

He pulled away from her and backed out of the room.

Her life was of interest to him now, but she was not the reason he was here.

In the hallway, he stopped in front of the eight by eleven school photo of the girl. *She* was his reason.

Maxim Kragen Jr., old man to the dead son, Maxim Kragen the III, wanted the child, his newly discovered grand-daughter. The dead son had been a sadistic bastard, but the old man? He was the prototype, and wielded real power. The power to take the sandy-skinned child smiling in the picture from this home and have her brought to him, was but one form.

Approaching the half-opened door of the child's room, he paused.

Frowning, he slipped inside, pressing the knife, hilt down, against the back of his forearm, out of sight for young eyes that may open in surprise or fright; but ready to sink into anyone that tried to interfere with his purpose.

The double-bed, illuminated by a night light, had the covers on one side pulled back.

It was empty.

He placed his hand on the exposed mattress and pillow where she had been. It was cool to the touch, which meant she'd left while ago.

He retreated from the room and cautiously stepped towards the one across the hall. The one at the end would be the last entered, but he had to be cautious as he eased inside the bedroom. The soft snores of the woman who'd worried about approaching the house earlier, was, as suspected, not sleeping alone. The bed was large, but not large enough for three.

The younger female was tucked against the older one's side, her small head resting against breast and shoulder, one knee bent on top of the older, browner, version of herself.

He walked around the foot of the bed and stood on the left, staring down at the woman. Her braless breasts were confined by a thin tank top. He pressed the tip of the blade against the base of the strap near the woman's cleavage, about to slice it away before remembering; that wasn't his purpose.

But her flesh, he wanted it exposed, bared to its raw brown beauty, offering itself for worship.

His eyes darted to the girl, and he frowned, realizing for the first time that life now had the potential to be constantly inconvenienced.

Suppressing a growl, he pressed the blade back against his forearm, bent low, inhaling the older version's breath as she expelled it. He breathed her into him, wrapping the warmth of her life essence around his heart before he decided to move on.

There was one more room.

He paused before leaving her, bent back down and pressed his lips against the woman's. Her eyes opened, but he didn't pull back.

She opened her mouth, and he kissed her deeper, his tongue slipping inside as she silently pulled more of his soul into her. Her eyes remained open the whole time. Seeing him. Seeing into him.

He pulled back and frowned at her.

He had a job to do. He couldn't let her distract him.

They never took their eyes off each other as he eased from the room, but he made sure to strategically keep his blade out of her line of sight. If she saw it, she would stop him, and this last stop had to be made.

Leaving the room, he continued down the hall to the door at the end. This door was closed. And it should be. It should've also been painted black to acknowledge what was taking place on the other side.

Entering the room, he shut the door swiftly, softly, firmly. He turned the lock so nothing could get out, or in. Pulling a second blade, he let both dance through his fingers, individual but syncopated. Their purpose? Paying homage to the shadow of death hovering on the other side of Mr. Jace's bed.

He looked from that shadow to the nearly dead man hooked up to machines that kept him breathing, his heart pumping, his brain barely firing. His spirit was ready to be untethered from the decomposing body that restrained it, but the machines hindered its ability. In the animal world, the natural world, Zeus wouldn't allow a good man to linger and suffer like this. He would sink his blade into the man's flesh and swiftly cut him free of this world. Wouldn't be vicious, wouldn't be bloody, wouldn't be a sacrifice. It would be a gift.

Light glinted off the blades twirling through his fingers, giving the illusion of electricity sparking from his fingers. One side of his mouth tilted upward as compulsion pulled him closer to the bed.

He had a debt to pay, and the Blade Spirits approved his actions.

Slowing the blade in his left hand, he laid it upon the older Black man's forehead. "See your enemies clearly in the next life."

He then placed the blade upon Mr. Jace's frail chest.

"You protected the child, kept her safe until you couldn't." He placed his hand on top of the blade, felt Mr. Jace's chest fall up and down. "Got a strong heart and spirit. And now you'll have protection in the spirit realm."

He lifted the blade off the dying man's chest and tucked it beneath his pillow. The two spirits would bind during the remainder of this life and Mr. Jace would be protected in the next.

Zeus wished the other man an easy passing and straightened. The spin of the blade in his right hand increased as he stared at the dense shadow.

"Be seeing you soon," he said before slipping from the room as silently as he'd entered.

Making his way down the hall and back down the stairs, he crept into the night and stalked the neighborhood with no plans to rest or sleep. He'd grown out of sleeping in unfamiliar places, with unfamiliar people, at a young age. Plus, he had a woman and child to keep safe. Bloodshed was on the horizon, the Blade Spirits foretold this; so, he stayed vigilant, stayed hunting; stalked through the night seeking which direction battle would come.

His blade's dance was euphoric as he hunted, its song humming through his soul, reminding him that he never moved through the night alone.

CHAPTER TWO

"Yes, I'm an old man but not so old that I'm above wanting the head and *the fucking cock* of the bastard that murdered my son," Maxim Kragen Jr. shouted, before comporting himself. "Do you understand the level of exposure and humiliation that butcher has cost me? And that *bitch*," he snarled, remembering the day his only child had brought that graceless cow into their home, fawning over her as if he was some enthralled servant.

Max and his wife had given their son everything he would ever need to one day take the reins of the Consortium's empire, but instead *she* had come along with her pretense of innocence, and taken their boy down a path of obsession that ultimately ended in his death.

"She's the reason my son is dead, the hand that pointed that killer towards your home. She's ultimately the one responsible for destroying the lives and livelihoods of over a fifth of our membership. I want them both dead. I want vengeance, Basir."

"Well, far be it for me to caution you towards patience," Basir Ahadi drawled from the computer screen. "But it's not like I'm not being sought after as a person of interest following the incident at my California home. And you shouldn't ignore the fact that your last attempt to avenge your son's murder ended with the deaths of two of your precious little cult members."

"Those deaths were not without purpose. If not for Cornelius' sacrifice I wouldn't have learned that my son fathered a child on that simpering bitch. And though she's tainted by her mother's genes, the last of my bloodline will be in my possession. I will have the life of my son's killer's, Basir, and you will help me, because despite all of our differences, it was me that gave you your cherished little pet."

Basir nodded at someone beyond the camera, then returned his attention to the screen. "You are careless with your power Maxim, and I have no illusion about your willingness to sacrifice, without reflection or care, anyone that is not you. I will not be sacrificed, my friend. Therefore, I must deny your request for my direct involvement in your search for vengeance. My life of hiding is the only sacrifice I am now willing to make for the Consortium."

Maxim didn't know where Basir was, but based on the setting sun and the distinctive blue waters in the background, he believed it was somewhere on the Mediterranean coast; likely in the same region that Zeus and a more hardened Sabrina would soon arrive in.

"I am however, willing to place at your disposable one of my most deadly servants," Basir continued. "He will kill for you, but is smart enough to kill *even* you, if that is what's needed to keep himself alive."

That was not the deal Max wanted.

Basir was known within the Algerian community in Marseille, the area where the woman and her killer were going. Basir's presence would open doors quickly, would ensure that Max had both protection and privileges extend to him once he arrived to watch justice handed down to Zeus and Sabrina. The same fucking people who were actively obstructing him from gaining possession of his grandchild.

His wife needed the distraction of the child, Maxim's child, to see that a part of their son still lived on.

"I would prefer you see to this personally," Max said sternly, tone brokering no room for discussion.

Basir laughed.

"I'm sure you would *prefer*, in the way that most Anglos...." Basir cleared his throat. Max wasn't fooled. "That most *Americans* do," Basir amended. "However, I've made your choices plain: my servant or my departure from the Consortium. Either way, I wish you well on your journey."

The day they diversified their membership for the sake of increased revenue and greater access to new markets, was the day the Consortium weakened their power structure. However, as planned, that money and access continued to prove beneficial.

"I accept your assistance," Max said. "Tell your man I'll meet him in two days at the Paris property; from there he will bring the child to the Chateau in Marseille and we will depart once the child is secured on my yacht. But before I leave for France, I have a small matter to look into here."

"I hope you find the resolution you seek, my friend. May divine blessings be upon you."

Basir ended the video call and Max stared at the blank screen wishing he could end Basir's life as easily. He may need the man now, but he would never forget that his son had been beheaded inside that man's home. That truth left a bitter hatred simmering in his heart. For now, he'd use Basir's assassin, and when his granddaughter was in his possession, he would root out Basir's location and notify the authorities, ensuring the safe capture of his dear, dear friend.

Sabrina sat in the backseat of the rental car with Briana's head tucked against her side, her niece's tears soaking through Sabrina's cotton T-shirt and bra. Bending her head, she wiped tears from her own eyes, not crying simply because Briana was crying, but because Briana was crying just like Sam used to. Silently, hiding her face so no one could see her pain.

It was selfish to take Bri away from the only family she knew.

Just because Sabrina was her blood, didn't mean it was best for Briana, not even if Sam and Mrs. Jace had determined that when the time was right, it would be.

Zeus watched her through the rearview mirror, the focus of his mercurial gaze assured her that she wasn't alone, but offered no indication on how a well-adjusted adult would lessen the child's grief.

"I don't know how to make it better," she said desperately to Zeus's reflection.

His eyes returned to the road, and she felt Bri take one of those triple breaths people deep in tears sometimes did. "Maybe it's best we take you back. We never should've taken you away, Zeus–"

Briana pulled away from her and looked at her with so much anger and betrayal in her tear-filled eyes Sabrina felt ashamed.

"I'm supposed to be with you! You just don't want me, you hate me, you don't care about me, nobody does!"

She was failing. Miserably.

"I do want you, but I also want what's best for you more than anything, even if that means what's best for you means that I'm not the one to take care of you."

"Everybody always says that. They say they want what's best for me but I'm always the one who has to suffer because of what they want. My mom wanted the best for me, so I never got to meet her. The Jaces want the best for me, so I can't be there for Mr. Jace when he's dying. He'll *live* for us, that's what he said. Now he's going to die. Everybody's going to let him die." She wiped her face and pulled away. "You want the best for me but all that really means is you already think I'm too much to deal with. Give me back. Fine. I don't need you. I don't need anybody."

Briana words and emotions slapped at Sabrina forcefully, repeatedly. She'd been so consumed with her fear of failing, that she'd simultaneously made Bri feel like she wasn't enough as well as too much.

Sabrina remembered how that felt, being not enough and too much, and it made her fight. And when fighting didn't help, she ran, left everything, and started the whole cycle over and over until she'd met the one person who chased her down and wouldn't let her go.

Zeus's eyes flicked towards her again and returned to the road.

Coward. Letting her get chewed up by her pint-sized mini me.

Fine. She wasn't perfect. Not a perfect woman, or perfect caregiver, or even a perfect partner. But she could be honest and love this little girl with all of her imperfect heart. The only person she'd allowed herself to love since losing Samantha was Zeus, and now here was Bri ripping through her heart, forcing it to grow, stretch, give more.

"Okay, I get it. You're angry and sad, and with everything that's going on I know you're scared as hell because I am too. My fear told me you'd be better off without me, and I shouldn't have listened to it because that hurt you. I apologize for that. Everything in me wants to protect you from hurt Bri, but like you said, even the best intentions can cause pain. So, I'll make a promise. Through good and bad, you're stuck with us. We'll make mistakes –"

"*She'll* make mistakes. She doesn't even make her bed. I am perfect," Zeus told Bri, finally having something to say.

Bri giggled, which made Sabrina's heart expand.

"*We* will make mistakes, all of us, and we'll get mad and–"

"I don't get mad," Zeus corrected. "Wasted energy."

Sabrina took a deep breath and closed her eyes for a moment, opened them, ignored Zeus and smiled at Bri. "Maybe we can discover together how we can make the blade wielding, selectively mute man mad."

Bri shook her head. "Nope, you're on your own there."

"Smart kid," Zeus said.

"Wow. The casual betrayal," Sabrina said, wiping drying tears from Briana's face. "I thought we were a sisterhood. Blood. Ride or dies."

"We are," Bri said, then motioned for Sabrina to lean down. "But I don't think it's good to make Zeus mad," she whispered.

Kid had a point, but even if Zeus was incensed, he'd never harm them.

"Don't worry, even if he was mad, you'd never know to look at him. Watch the blades, the way they move will always let you know what's going on if you can read them right. Ultimately what I am saying is that we'll always be with you."

"Even in death," Zeus stated, from the front.

"*Kind* of creepy," Bri muttered.

"Yes," Sabrina said, wanted to smack Zeus in the back of the head. "Yes, it is. But I'll keep it real. In this family, creepiness will be the least of your problems."

Which is what made Sabrina afraid for Briana the most. Knowing what true evil was, knowing that it knew who Briana was, and would inevitably attempt to take her away from them.

In Maxim's impatience, he arrived at the house an hour earlier than anticipated. He told Alden to park across the street and two houses up from the home of Mr. and Mrs. Jace. His intention was to speak with the couple in person. He didn't want anyone else to know the intimate details concerning his son's child, but *he* needed to understand why she had been fostered with this couple, instead of raised by her mother. He'd learned that Sabrina had a history of associating with drug dealers, couldn't maintain regular employment, cohabitated with murderers, and rolled across America like a human tumbleweed, unstable, her fate determined by the direction of the wind. It was for the best that she didn't raise his grandchild, but he had to know the details. To use them against her if the battle for his grandchild went through the courts, he would need any leverage he could get.

"It appears there's been a death," Maxim reflected.

He was seated behind Alden on the driver's side, and through the tinted black window, he watched a constant stream of people bringing food and flowers to the Jaces' home.

After nearly two hours of waiting, Alden cleared his throat. "The plane is scheduled to depart in less than an hour sir; we'll need to leave soon if we are to arrive on time."

"The plane leaves when I say it leaves," Max snapped. "Call ahead and tell them we've been delayed."

"Yes, sir."

The sun began to set an hour later.

An older woman came out of the house and sat heavily in one of the rocking chairs. It seemed the last of the visitors had departed. The woman's grief wrapped around her like a shawl. He felt the weight of it even from here. His family had lost so much with their Maxim's death. Whatever loss the woman felt couldn't compare, but he acknowledged that she felt it. These people grew used to losing family and friends, it made their grief more bearable than his.

"I'll return shortly," Max told Alden.

"Sir..."

Max got out of the car, straightened his suit jacket, and approached the house. The woman didn't even register his presence until he was at the foot of the brick steps.

When she looked at him, her gaze seemed perplexed, weary. She remained silent.

"Hello, Mrs. Jace. It is Mrs. Jace, isn't it?"

"It's been a long day mister, and I have no patience for questions or conversation. If you'd kindly get off my property, we can avoid any undue drama."

"I have a feeling you know who I am and why I'm here, so I'll cut to the chase. I know the child has left with her mother and her mother's lover, perhaps to give you time and space to grieve? Perhaps to keep my grandchild away from me?" He shrugged. "It's no matter, it's you I would like to gather information from, since my granddaughter has lived her whole life in your care."

"Hey asshole, the Señora, she's not taking interviews. Walk away my friend, walk while you still have two pale spindly legs to walk on."

Max looked towards the screen door, surprised. The interior of the house was dark, as were the clothes of the speaker who was mostly a silhouette, a pale face mostly hidden behind black shades. He was perhaps six feet, and until Max heard the distinctive click of a magazine being inserted into a long weapon, he would've believed him a visitor who'd overstayed his welcome.

"Is he one of them?" Max asked the old woman, certain the man was a part of the group of people responsible for harboring his son's killer, as well as for the deaths of Delilah and Cornelius, two members of the religious order he'd founded in Ireland.

"I'm Juarez, a man like no other," the shadow man said. "Which means I can shoot you and your car butler through the heart from a mile away."

Max's face burned with indignation. He had a plane to catch, and a granddaughter to acquire. No time for shootouts in suburbia with no one, not even his driver, aware of the danger he faced.

"Mrs. Jace, perhaps I can speak to you at a later time, maybe when you're in a better frame of mind?"

"If we see you around here again my friend," the man in the house replied instead, all the boastfulness gone. "There will be no words, and no warnings, motherfucker."

Max walked back to the car without replying

Alden rushed from the car open the door.

"All these... *people* and their lack of deference," he seethed. There was a time when they knew to fear and revere men like him. These days they consider themselves equal or better, and that needed to end.

If the Consortium wielded the power it had less than a year ago, he would've ensured that that woman's whole house had been raised to the ground, but the setbacks and losses the organization faced left many of them exposed and without the resources they once had.

"Were you able to acquire the information you needed, Sir?" Alden asked, as he maneuvered the car back towards the freeway.

If he trusted his luck, Maxim would've struck his impertinent driver in the back of the head.

He would not play the games of simple men, becoming frustrated by present circumstances. No, instead he would plan for a future that saw the Consortium strong, moving offensively instead of defensively once he had his little tainted descendent fully within his control.

CHAPTER THREE

They landed in Charles De Galle because Zeus wanted his woman and her.... He was going to say her mini-me, but that would mean Briana was just Sabrina's. She was his, but his what?

He frowned.

Not his daughter, he didn't have permission for that title yet.

His charge? No, she was more than a responsibility.

His dependent? Nah.

He stopped in the middle of the concourse and stared at... his girl? No.

He watched Bri and Sabrina walk ahead, talking with animation and excitement despite it being nearly midnight. They spoke half the flight here. They should've been tired of speaking because he was tired of listening to them speak. But like magic, their words kept materializing.

His niece? He shook his head.

Something more. Maybe he'd–

Someone ran into him from behind. He shifted around, his hummingbird blade in his hand instantly, and it made thirteen imperceptible cuts along the man's chest, torso, back, abdomen, before Zeus decided it was okay to stop.

The concourse was nearly empty. There was plenty of space to avoid him, but the man had been so busy disparaging the flight attendants, he didn't pay attention to where he was going.

The man was incensed, didn't know he'd been wounded multiple times and wouldn't until much later. He cursed Zeus in French and righted his luggage, shaking his fist in Zeus's face then attempted to walk around him. Zeus grabbed the man by his throat and pulled him closer.

Parisians are the *worst,* the voice in his head mimicked Bri.

The condescending little shit. That thought was his own.

"You're little," Zeus told the man. "But you squawk too loud. Learn to shut the fuck up and pay attention, or next time a hummingbird will come along and cut out your tongue." He closed his eyes and sighed, pulled the man closer and breathed in the sour scent beneath the expensive cologne. "No one wants to hear you. Shut up," he said, tightening his hold and opening his eyes.

He half-smiled when he saw the woman and child running towards him. He didn't want them to think he was doing something wrong, which he wasn't, the appreciative gazes of the passing attendants told him so. All he'd wanted was space to walk and contemplated what he would call Bri, and the man turning purple in his grasp had interfered with that.

"Let him go Zeus."

"We're old friends," Zeus assured her. "Catching up."

Neither Sabrina nor Bri spoke enough French to know what the man was struggling to say.

"Well, can you catch up without your fingers wrapped around his *throat?*"

"Yes," he said, as Sabrina attempted to pry them from the man's neck. She always smelled good, he leaned closer wanting to taste her.

"No," she muttered.

He released the man's throat but held him in place with his gaze.

"In English," Zeus said in French. "So they understand. Tell them we're friends."

"Mais oui! Mon Bon amie! My very, very, good friend, yes," the man rushed out. "Je suis désolé." He bowed to Sabrina and Bri and nearly sprinted away.

Sabrina gave Zeus that look that said, *we're going to have words later.*

Briana grabbed his hand and held it. "So, you won't get into any more trouble," she consoled, patting his hand apologetically.

Bright kid, he thought looking at Sabrina beneath hooded eye. *She* was the trouble.

He picked Briana up and carried her.

"Zeus, she can walk."

"But I don't have to if you want to carry me," Briana told him, wrapping her arms around his neck.

He smirked at Sabrina.

"You two are going to get on my *last* nerve," she said, glaring. But her anger wasn't real. Her eyes reflected too much joy, and he was highly attuned to her joy, was growing addicted to it because it paired surprisingly well with his more violent compulsions.

"What's your favorite part of Paris?" Bri asked him after

they made it through customs, claimed their luggage, and approached the SUV rental.

When St. Catherine's orphanage had been in Paris, before permanently relocating to the US, he'd spent hours walking the canals and the parks. Nature calmed him, but mundane Parisian walkways had been too tame for his wild spirits.

"The catacombs," he eventually said.

Dark was soothing. The dead, death, was soothing.

He wondered if the Frenchman who'd bumped into him had realized that the stinging of his flesh was from razon thin cuts that, if he were not more careful, could've ended in death and darkness.

"Okay, that's kind of weird," Bri said, climbing into the back seat of the SUV and reaching for Sabrina's phone. "Look up catacombs," she directed the device as he and Sabrina loaded the trunk.

"Catacombs are better than the Eiffel Tower," he informed her, as he drove from the airport.

"Nuh-uh! Take us to the Eiffel Tower now and I'll show you."

"It's after one in the morning," Sabina stepped in. "You need to sleep Briana."

"I'm too excited to sleep!" The child laughed.

"Drama queen much?" Sabrina smiled.

But it's what Zeus felt too. Excitement. No blades in hand, no body to carve through, but he felt it, Briana's, Sabrina's... and he wanted to give them this. Wanted to warm himself by the light of their happiness as he shared the city that he never really liked.

"I won't sleep 'til we reach the house," he said. "Let's skip the hotel. I can show you Paris by night." In the darkness was the best way to see it. "We'll watch the sunrise from the steps of the Sacré Coeur, get breakfast, then head south. We'll make it home before noon."

"Are you up for an all-nighter, miss 'I'm too excited'?"

"Yes m'am," Briana said sweetly.

"Look at that politeness," Sabrina said, then turned back to Zeus. "If you weren't driving right now, I would kiss you."

He glanced at her. "Kiss me anyway."

She leaned over, her lips soft and warm against the edge of his jaw. "I love you Big Man. Now let's do this."

He remained aware of the road, focused on getting them to their destination, but inside, that feeling inside his chest made him feel as invincible as the God who shared his name. But what he felt for this woman was big enough to uproot heaven and earth, he could create a whole new realm of existence, level everything within a hundred-mile radius to rubble if he were to set it free.

He reached over and rested his hand on her thigh and moved his fingers in a leisurely dance.

"I love you too, Big Man," Briana parroted from the backseat.

He reached back and grab her foot and she squealed.

The edge of his mouth tilted up.

This was his family.

The woman Sabrina wanted him to meet, she might have been blood, but she wasn't family. But for his woman, he'd exhaust all the possibilities, all opportunities, to be given the love that he may have missed. For the opportunity to be claimed by his blood, to knowing his heritage. He wanted to see her, the woman who gave birth to him, but he could stalk her from afar. This reunion wouldn't change anything, wouldn't make him want more than what he now had. But love meant giving people the opportunity to see the truth you already knew existed. So, he would meet the woman who left him to live or die – and he did both – in the care of the church. And unlike Bri, the ones who raised him were nothing like the Jaces.

Sabrina's fingers wrapped around his, stopping their dance, and rested them against her thigh again.

"We're just leaving no stone unturned," she promised. "I want you to have all the answers, all the love, even if mine and Bri's seem like enough."

"Is there a way for you to direct some of this love into making the bed in the morning?" he asked, curiously. Maybe that was the motivation she needed.

"Really? Do you want to go there? *Now?*"

Hell no he didn't, not if it was going to lead to conflict.

Her response told him that it would be.

"If we did go there, you'd probably miss that," he nodded ahead towards the Arc de Triumph.

He wished for noise cancelling headphones as their excitement reached dog whistle levels of shrieking.

Fucking Paris.

"Let them settle, Almaya," Terry chided. Pulling his shirt over his head. "They're probably in the hotel sleeping–"

"Zeus isn't sleeping. Zeus roams unfamiliar spaces, he's hyper-vigilant, more so now that he has a family under threat. That man ain't sleeping!"

"So, you think he's going to call you because he's *awake?*"

"Hell no," she said, begrudgingly. "But dammit...."

She unwound the cut up t-shirt she used as a towel from

around her locs, and they fell over her shoulders and down her neck, back, and breast like a mantle of responsibility.

A man, a man she had allowed on her mountain, around *her* Brood, lost his life, and though no one else had been severely injured, they *could* have been.

Almaya had a right to worry.

The Consortium targeted them not only because Zeus killed Kragen III, but because the whole sick organization was being exposed and dismantled bit by bit. Her Brood was cutting off their money supply, exposing their perversions and illegal activities, getting those motherfuckers indicted left and right, and Almaya loved every fucking minute of it.

But men with power, on the brink of losing that power, were like wounded animals who felt death coming and were forced to fight harder, becoming more vicious to avoid their end.

Terry's arms circled her from behind and Almaya tilted her head to the side, smiled as his lips pressed against her neck.

This man... her soul's light, the earth she rooted in, her voice of reason when she was being unreasonable.

She smiled wider, remembering their first encounter.

She never would've imagined all those years ago that they would end up like this.

But he had.

"Are you regretting your decision to let Zeus and Sabrina go to France alone?"

She snorted. "No."

Their swaying side to side motion stopped.

"What did you do?"

She turned in his arms.

Never was there a more beautiful man to walk this earth than her mind warrior.

"I love you," she smiled with earnest.

He bent down, pressed his lips to hers and lifted her much softer form, his large hands palming each naked globe of her ass as she wrapped her legs around his hips.

"What did you do?" he asked, undeterred.

She narrowed her gaze and hopped down.

"The request was unreasonable," she said, walking to the bed to grab her bra. "And sometimes I am forced to be the voice of reason."

He waited.

She shrugged and dressed in an old pair of jeans and a ratty T-shirt that wouldn't be ruined by the repairs still to be done in the bar.

He waited.

"Well, I was right about the Jaces wasn't I?" she reminded him. "Imagine what could've happened if I didn't have Juarez at the house the minute Zeus and Sabrina left. And the fact that that hateful evil son of a bitch went there in person...."

"What did you do, Almaya?"

"We just had sex Terry; you should be nicer to me right now."

He ran his fingers through his hair, winding the thick mass into a knot at the nape of his neck, like a black woman - or in this case a Choctaw - getting ready to fight.

"I contacted Carl," she stated quickly.

Terry looked at her and she could feel his cool disappointment brushing against her skin.

"He's not one of ours, May. He's not Brood for a reason."

"Well, he's *mine*." Carl was someone she feared they would never agree on, because Terry's code of ethics was much more developed than hers.

"He promised me he'd watch them from afar. Unless he was needed."

"And did you consider what would happen if Zeus and Carl come in to contact with each other?"

She had.

Under the wrong circumstances, it would be vicious, and it would be bloody, and one of them would likely die.

"Carl knows how to hide like no other," she assured.

"And Zeus knows how to seek like no other."

She walked to the bedroom door.

"I promised Zeus and Sabrina that the Brood wouldn't intrude on this reunion and they won't. I trust Carl," she said, and left the room.

Walking up the stairs that led up through many levels of the complex, she exited on the first floor where Mama's House stood in stages of repair. Her actions weighed heavily on her fifty-eight-year-old body.

Sometimes her gut reactions were all she had. She prayed that trusting her gut this time wouldn't result in more pain and more loss, the way it had with Cornelius.

They sat on the stairs stacked like Russian nesting dolls. Zeus sat behind Sabrina, tucked between the warmth of his hard thighs, and Briana slept between the juncture of Sabrina's thighs. Just moments before, Bri had partly danced, partly ran, from the grass to the stairs below the Cathedral, where they now sat.

Sabrina sipped on her chocolat chaud and took another bite out of her croissant, before handing it up to Zeus, settling deeper into him.

"If someone had said, on the night we met in that warehouse, 'don't worry Sabrina, in less than two months you'll love this blood-soaked man and watch the sunrise from the steps of the Sacré Coeur Basilica with your sister's daughter', I would've cussed them out and called them the devil."

Zeus grunted.

"I would've killed him."

"Why would you kill somebody for predicting that you and me would end up in France?" She laughed. If anyone overheard them, they'd think Zeus was using dark humor when in reality, he was simply being honest. There was a time when his honesty, would've sent her running. Those times were long gone.

"I'd kill them because they told me my future, not because of what the future held. If they knew about this, what else would they know, and when would they use it against me? Kill 'em," he shrugged. "Never have to wonder."

She learned further back and frowned at him, wanting him to think about more humane options. They had a kid now.

She opened her mouth to say that, but he swooped down and pressed his lips to hers, kissing her so deeply she forgot what the hell she was going to fuss about it.

It has been two days and she missed the morning ritual that had been his before she'd adopted it as her own. And these days she needed their ritual as much as he did.

Was she bad for wanting to lay Bri on the concrete, crawl onto his lap, straddle him and—

Zeus pulled away.

"Don't feel bad for the made-up dead psychic. If they had good intentions, they would've kept their predictions to themselves. They would've known I would kill them if they were truly wise anyway. But they chose to flex their power.

With me. Death is the only answer to that. The spirits say it's so."

She snorted. "Bullshit, *you* say it's so."

"My words are their words," he said sagely.

She laughed again. He was so full of shit.

"Be still woman, you'll wake up Bri. This is our alone time."

He really was romantic... In some lost chamber of his morbid heart.

She settled back into him, brushing a straight curl from Briana's forehead. She wondered if Zeus felt any of the trepidation she had about reuniting with his family. It was strange. The more they were with the Brood, the less interest he had in meeting his blood family. As far as families went, the Brood were Zeus's.

"Why do you think with all the cultural variations within the Brood, Mama never included a Black woman on the team?"

He grunted, but it was a few minutes before he responded. "Bride's Black Irish, that should count."

Sabrina rolled her eyes. Bride having waves of black hair and Irish ancestry did not a Black woman make. And she was the only female Brood Mate, but she had as much, if not more, big dick, anti-social energy than most of the men. Bride had become like a second best-friend by association... if one could be friends with a vicious fairy-looking Fury.

"Also, unlike you, Mama likes an orderly house. You don't even make your bed. Why chance another Black woman that won't make her bed in the house like you?"

She was about to get up and cuss him out about making that fucking bed, but he pointed off into the distance and she saw the faint purpling in the black sky.

"Wake her," Zeus said. "It's time."

Sabrina smiled and bent over, smooching Briana all over her face until she stirred.

"Wake up sleepy head, or you're going to miss the main event."

Bri yawned. Loudly. And stretched all over Sabrina, then stood and kissed her before walking up the two steps to kiss Zeus, and lean against his back, wrapping her arms around his neck as she rested her head against his shoulder.

"I had a bad dream," Sabrina heard her whisper to Zeus. "But I saw you in the dark and at first I thought you were a monster, but I heard you say, 'you're mine, mean's you're protected'. Then arms wrapped around me, and I felt safe, and I knew nothing bad could get to me, and I wasn't scared anymore."

Sabrina's chest tightened.

It was hard to pull air into her lungs as the memory of being pinned down by Maxim Kragen III – Briana's father – flashed through her body and mind.

But Zeus had found her, destroyed the evil housed in the body of a madman. She didn't want Bri to ever experience that kind of terror, but because of who her father was, who her grandfather was, she didn't have the luxury of living like the threats weren't real. If Briana was ever in trouble, Zeus would protect her. She would protect her.

"Be still," Zeus demanded, his fingers dancing against her abdomen, tapping away her brief panic.

She focused on the beauty of the rising sun, Zeus and Bri and Paris tethering her to right now. She breathed in Zeus's clarifying sense of purpose, rooted in his sharp metal and foresty earth smell, and where Bri hugged him from behind, he held every part of her, reminding her that unlike all the times before him, she didn't have to face the dangers of the future alone.

"The Blade spirits..." he said to Briana. "They speak to you when you're asleep. That's how it begins. They show you that sometimes the things that look like monsters are monsters, and sometimes things become monsters to protect you. The Blade spirits showed you that even if I have to become a monster, I'll protect you."

He really was God, man, and monster.

"That was amazing," Bri whispered. "I don't think you've ever said so many words at once. *Ever*. I didn't think you could."

Sabrina's laughter rang out over the city with the force of lightning, but filled with more love than a thousand church bells tolling.

"Blades do the talking. I do the ki–"

"Sooo," Sabrina interrupted before he really freaked Bri out. "Since the Blade spirits showed Bri the future. Doesn't that make her, by your earlier reasoning, a psychic?"

His mercurial eyes glinted.

He didn't like being reminded of his earlier words.

She smiled wide.

"You're not as clever as you think you are." That's all he said, and she felt like she'd finally gained the upper hand.

She settled smugly between his thighs and watched as the day came into being.

It was the most beautifully dramatic sunrise she'd ever seen. And she was here with the Parisian panoramic stretched out below and around them.

"This night has been wonderful," she said standing, bent over, and held Zeus's head in her hands and kissed him. "Behave," she warned and pulled away as he tried to deepen the kiss. "As beautiful as Paris is, it's time to get you two home. I'll drive, you rest," she told Zeus, making it her mission to show him that he was equally as loved and cared for. No matter what happened with his family, no matter what happened with Kragen Jr, he was hers to watch over as surely as Briana was.

Sabrina couldn't protect Sam, couldn't protect their mother from herself, but she was willing to die so these two could live.

~

He didn't rest.

He gritted his teeth as they wound through the narrow curves, the coastal air buffeting the SUV possibly the only thing keeping them from going over the edge.

Terry told him before they'd left Mama's House, *pick your battles,* so Zeus didn't caution her or suggest he drive the rest of the way, because his woman was vengeful and would probably drive faster.

He looked over his shoulder and saw that Briana was awake again, watching a video on her iPad, with Sabrina's wireless earbuds in her ears.

Both of them were so unconcerned.

"Sharp curve coming," he said. *Inform*, Terry said, *don't demand.* "We'll go over the side of the mountain if we keep on as we are." *We*, so she didn't feel singled out. He'd be a fucking mind hunter too, by the time this trip was over.

Sabrina slowed just as a produce truck rounded the mountain towards them, nearly crowding them off the road.

She flipped the driver off and muttered "asshole", under her breath as if it had been his fault. She drove at a more sedate pace the rest of the way down the mountainous curves.

"Never again," he informed her, just in case she was under the illusion that he'd ever let her drive while they were in Europe.

"I slowed down," she said defensively.

He didn't give a shit.

She wasn't a naturally cautious driver. He wanted her to be, control and discipline saved him. She was impulsive in moments of high emotion. It was true when they met, and it was true now. Loving her meant accepting her challenges as she accepted his.... even if his challenges only existed in her mind.

They approached the small town he called home at least once a year. He scanned the faces they passed, noticing which buildings had changed within the ten months since he'd last been here, and which remained the same. Most all of them were the same.

Although the town was more rustic, more sedate, than Marseille, it was more home to him than the place he was born. Though twenty minutes outside the second largest city in France, it was not crowded with people, smells, and sounds.

The average age in the seaside town was above forty, but younger families had started moving to the lower lying areas once the developers and newer restaurants and businesses had begun building up the area over the last ten years.

Zeus wondered if any of his neighbors would recognize him now. He felt brand new.

"The road to my villa is up a bit and then to the left," he said before the navigation system did.

Briana put her tablet down and looked out the window, watching them pass through streets surrounded by businesses and buildings that had been here for hundreds of years. His place sat overlooking a cliff at the end of the road, his closest neighbors about one hundred and fifty feet downhill.

Sabrina drove the car up the stone path that led to the house, put the car in park, and stared.

"Huhn," she uttered.

He scanned the area, stepped outside.

"Stay in the car."

He walked the perimeter of the house, checked for any signs of disturbance at the windows and doors, and searched the ground and foliage for any signs of recent activity. Moving along the stone wall that separated his land from the neighbors down the hill and provided a barrier between his property and the cliff below it.

Entering the house through the side door. He felt the vibration of his watch. He went inside the kitchen pantry and opened what looked like an old fuse box, disarming the old school alarm system which alerted him if the windows or doors had been breached.

He walked through the rooms on the first and second floor, then went down to his workspace in the cellar, checking everything there before going back upstairs and sealing the hidden wall entrance, then made his way to the front door.

Sabrina and Briana got out the moment they saw him, Briana raced towards him and Sabrina went to the back of the SUV and began pulling out luggage.

"Bathroom?" Bri shouted.

He pointed to the water closet with toilet and sink, just to the right of the door.

As she ran past him, he grabbed the heavier bags, leaving Sabrina the groceries they'd stopped to buy in Lyon.

He placed his and Sabrina's bags in the larger bedroom

downstairs and took Bri's to the larger of the two bedrooms upstairs. When he got back to the kitchen, Sabrina had discovered where to store the food and cleaning supplies.

He watched her as she moved about. The last time they'd been alone in the bed had been the last time they'd fucked, the last time he'd slept.

He watched her walk over to the door of the pantry, and when she stepped inside, he followed her in and closed the door.

She looked over her shoulder as the door clicked and her smile was knowing as she backed up, the back of the pantry wall stopped her retreat.

"No," she warned, pointing her finger at him as if he was a misbehaving dog.

He lowered his head and growled, the edge of his mouth tilted, in anticipation.

She felt like prey. His prey. Her capture too long in coming.

"I was patient."

She nodded as he pressed against her, lowering his head.

"You were," she breathed. "I just need —"

"*I* need," he said, lips brushing against her much softer, much sweeter mouth. He bit her lower lip softly, circled it. "I *need*." He said again, rougher. He gripped the back of her head, crushing her two-strand twist in his fist and forcing her head farther back.

"Take what you need Zeus," she whispered. "You deserve it, and it's yours."

His.

He crushed his mouth to hers. His tongue desperate to taste, to press against all those parts of her, to discover the new tastes of her, it changed each time they kissed, sometimes more salty, sometimes more sweet, more bitter, more tart, more spicy. Each time different. Each time a discovery.

Their tongues were greedy for each other, and his knew each place to press, to slide against, to breathe into to make her soften, cracking open the shell of her control, making her soften in that way which made her limbs barely functional, forcing him to grip the back of her ass and mold her legs around his hips so that she wouldn't slide to the ground in an ungraceful heap.

She ground against his cargo pant clad erection, wrapping her arms around his neck, gripping his head so desperately he could feel her short round nails sink into his scalp.

He slid his hand in the pocket of space between their bodies and wrestled the elastic material of her leggings over her waist and down to the base of her ass. Sliding his fingers into the pool of slippery liquid warming her entrance, he dipped in and out, circling and massaging her clit until she cried out, pulled her mouth from his and dipped her head, focused on unbuttoning and unzipping his pants. When she reached inside and fisted his dick, he froze, a rumble rolling around in his chest.

He needed. Needed her like fire needed oxygen. Needed but couldn't have. After three fucking days, he still couldn't have the release he needed.

"What? What's wrong?" she panted.

He'd heard the bathroom door open and little feet making their way towards them, even if she didn't.

"Hey!" Briana called out. "Where are you guys; where is everybody?"

Panicked, Sabrina pushed him away, pulled up her pants and adjusted her clothes.

"I got this," she told Zeus, making her way to the door.

"Don't come out 'til you're..." she waved towards his half-exposed erection. "Presentable."

He'd be in here for-fucking-ever then, he thought, glaring at the door she'd escaped through. Tucking himself back into his pants, he crouched down and removed his favorite blade from the sheath secured against his calf. The blade moved through his fingers at an increasingly fast clip.

He'd been good, compromised, been patient, listened, smiled. Sort of.

He pulled the Fairbain stylus resting against his back and encouraged it to dance too. As if with a mind of their own, the two blades moved in unison. His black soul blade was the dark and his Bowie, a silver moon dispersing the dark residue of his soul blade.

The blades' motions reached a crescendo then stopped abruptly and Zeus panted, the muscles in his arms and fingers tingled with energy. He threw the blades and they lodged in the floor, each tip buried exactly half an inch into the pantry's wooden floor, a hair outside of each foot.

Too long.

He ground his molars.

He'd gone too fucking long without his morning ritual. He needed it for balance now, needed it to control the compulsions. *Fuck or hunt.* He hadn't had the satisfaction of successfully completing either lately.

The Blade Spirits sent a battery of images through his mind. *A blade slicing through pale distended flesh, no blood. A blade severing a throat, axe chopping off a head, a blade serrating flesh.*

He exhaled in satisfaction, the images diminishing the pull of the compulsions.

He breathed in, practically smelling iron-heavy blood. Took another breath and smiled.

Yes, he needed the kill of a hunt, needed to fuck, but the Blade Spirits reminded him that he needed something else just as bad. And he had it.

On the other side of the door, where Sabrina and Bri were laughing and singing.

Sabrina wasn't a good singer.

Briana was worse.

He shook his head, pulled his blades from the floor, and secured them so Bri wouldn't see them. His training taught her they were there, waiting. Everyone who knew him knew they were there. Luckily not a lot of people knew him.

Slipping quietly from the pantry, he watched them cook.

When they noticed him, they came over and sang to and around him, Bri hugging him briefly, Sabrina, kissing him once, twice.

The compulsions faded to a quiet hum, as his heart swelled with what he increasingly recognized as love. But the word felt too weak to describe what continued to grow inside his chest. He hadn't known hearts could literally grow, but he could feel it squirming around in their love, trust, and acceptance.

He kissed Sabrina, breathed her. His woman.

She knew who he was, knew what he was, knew how he was.

He stared at her and she no longer freaked out over his unwavering, unblinking attention; she'd grown used to his silent worship.

Winking at him, she continued to do what she was doing when he'd entered. Making a mess of his kitchen.

Protect Our gifts, the Blade Spirits whispered.

Zeus strode through the kitchen, exiting the house at the back door. Moving through the neighborhood, he refamiliarized himself with the scents, the people, the nuances. He checked the perimeter of his land where he'd hidden things to lay in wait for intruders. Took the time to remove or disable most, Bri would want to run and explore. It took two hours, but once he returned to the house, he was certain that for tonight no one was hiding in the dark, waiting to attack.

"Everything okay?" Sabrina asked.

He washed his hands and sat at the table next to the plate where three homemade burgers and half a plate of reheated fries were placed. Briana sat across from him reading.

"It's good," he said, confirming there was no immediate threat. "Burgers over-cooked though."

"Told you," Bri chimed in, never taking her eyes off her book.

"Hush Ms. Smarty Pants," Sabrina swatted at Bri. "And you," she pointed a warning finger at him. "You eat the burger and say thank you."

He ate silently, knowing he wasn't thankful for this dry-assed burger. When he was done, he cleaned his dishes, left the kitchen, and roamed the interior of the house. This time checking and rechecking entry points, boobytraps....

"Enough," Sabrina said, stepping in front of him at the bottom of the stairs. "Enough," she repeated. He came to a stop. "I'm not about to let you continue running yourself ragged."

She grabbed his hand and took him to the bathroom as Briana went into their bedroom and climbed on the bed.

He frowned at her. She had her own bed to sleep in now, he wanted to tell her.

In the bathroom, he watched Sabrina curiously as she stripped him and nudged him towards the shower, where she cleaned him as if he were her second child. He tried to catch her gaze, but she avoided his eyes. Instead, her hands worked all around his body.... and she wasn't gentle... and it wasn't sexy. She wasn't a naturally domestic type.

"I ate the burgers," he pointed out rationally. Sometimes calm reason worked, sometimes he had to let her woman's brain run its course.

"I don't care about a damn burger," she snapped.

Woman's brain wins.

She grabbed a towel and dried him vigorously, left the bathroom and returned with his linen drawstring sleeping pants, and a t-shirt, which meant Briana would be sleeping in their bed another night.

"The house is safe," he offered. He'd check again if it helped her feel they were safe.

"I know it is, but you're *not* superman."

"No, I'm a god," he dared, which made her shake her head.

"You're a *man*, Zeus, and you haven't slept, you haven't even really rested in days. Baby, you need to rest," she said, and the love and worry in her eyes made his heart beat faster. Cradling his head, she kissed him and pulled away before he could tempt her into more.

"I could check one more time," he told her, wanting her to know he could keep her safe, that he would never let another steal her away from him and try to violate her again.

She gripped his hand and pulled him towards their bedroom, her look daring him not to follow.

Briana scooted to the other side of the bed as Sabrina pulled back the bedsheets, motioning for Zeus to lay down. He obeyed the silent demand, choosing to forgo any conversation about security checks, because he knew that would spark her temper and he didn't feel like dealing with it.

Laying back, he settled against the pillow and Briana

moved closer to him, laying her head against his right shoulder. Sabrina got in bed and molded her body against his left side.

"Sleep Big Man," Sabrina whispered. "We've got you."

He lay there staring up at the shadowed ceiling feeling slightly smothered, but it was tolerable. It felt right to be surrounded by their love.

He forgot sometimes, to stop, to sleep. Not having his routines made it worse, not being able to release his urges made it worse. This is what Sabrina was upset about then. She didn't fear for her safety, she was concerned about his well-being.

"Sleep Zeus," Sabrina whispered, stroking his chest.

He closed his eyes.

His mind immediately returned to the hotel room explosion that ended in Sabrina being taken from him. It flashed to her fighting Kragen for her life.

Now that he knew what it meant to be loved, if he lost her, lost *them*, there would be no escaping. He'd lose the decades of control the Blade Spirits had cultivated and, in its place, there would exist a rabid beast, a true monster. He didn't want to unleash that kind of suffering into the world, but he would, he thought relinquishing his mind to the shadows of sleep, he would.

CHAPTER FOUR

B asir's man stood at Max's door, scowling like a goon.

Max didn't want to allow him in; and it wasn't because he didn't want a North African in his living quarters; he socialized regularly with people he wouldn't choose to interact with under normal circumstances. No, he didn't want to invite this particular man in because of the look in his eyes.

The tranquilized animal counting the moments before the chemical paralytic wore off so that it could rip out your throat look.

The man would do quite nicely as an executioner, but as a guest.... Max restrained himself from curling his nose in distaste and opened the door wider, letting Basir's assassin inside.

The man stepped through the door and scanned the area with such detail Max felt as if his bones had been picked through. Clearing his throat, he took control of the situation.

"Thank you for coming," he said, politely. "Would you like a drink?"

"It is against my religion," the man said, his voice cultured, yet unsurprisingly accented.

He couldn't simply say, no? Max thought, walking to the mini bar.

"Would you like water then?"

"No."

His rudeness was intolerable.

The assassin watched him beneath hooded eyes. It was as if he couldn't comprehend the level of power Max held, and therefore didn't act accordingly.

"I take it Basir informed you of the nature of your assignment?"

"I am here."

The sooner he got this person away from him and on the job, the sooner he could focus on making the child's special room. He would need a secluded space to help her learn to accept his new role in her life. It would be a place to... not break her, but train her, so that she accompanied him willingly, docilely. He could not abide spirited children and the colored ones, they were irritatingly so.

Once his Bourbon was in hand, Max picked up a folder and walked it to Basir's assassin, making a jest of handing him the bourbon before laughing and handing him the folder.

"This is where they are located," he informed the assassin. "The child is not to be harmed," he emphasized. "Bring her straight to my yacht. The man...do your unmitigated worst. The woman...break her then dispose of her."

A spark of light flickered in the assassin's dark eyes. Max was uncertain if it was the former or latter order that stirred the assassin's interest. He smiled inwardly. Every man – sinner, sinister, and saint –had their vices.

Scanning through the meager folder, Basir's man studied the photos of Zeus, Sabrina, and, though it pained him to acknowledge the relationship, his grandchild Briana. The folder contained their location but there was no information to be found on any known associates or relatives in the area, which led Max to conclude the pair brought the child here to hide.

That they had the audacity to believe they could live a simple happy life hidden away in Southern France after the destruction they'd caused, would soon turn into a lesson about how the world really worked.

Handing the folder back to Maxim, the assassin nodded. "I will bring the child to your ship within your seventy-two hours."

"Bring photos of their bodies," Maxim added, wanting to be there, to watch their destruction. But he'd have to settle for the next best thing. He couldn't afford to be caught embroiled in another murder investigation. "If you need to contact me before you deliver the child, I will be at the Chateau in Marseille tomorrow."

Basir's man left as silently as he'd come, but the heaviness of his presence remained. Maxim opened the balcony doors overlooking the Seine, and looked out on the Paris skyline, contemplating ways he could use the next few hours to bring a new energy into the space.

"I really should call the wife," he uttered; she would want to know about his progress. He called the concierge instead. When the man asked how he could be of service, Maxim said one word. "Alabaster."

"Oui, Monsieur, the product will be delivered to you shortly."

Maxim disconnected the call, showered, and dressed in

black silk lounge pants with matching robe. He was waiting
for the new arrival when his cell phone rang.

"Ah," he answered, smiling. "The Good Shephard. How
are you Duval?"

"How do you imagine Maxim? How should one *be* after
he's learned his only daughter is dead?"

Which is one of the reasons Max hadn't contacted the
Shepherd for this assignment. Not only had the two members
of the Shepherd's flock bungled the assignment, but they also
had the temerity to die in the process. Luckily, this *Mama's
Brood* organization, which had given refuge to his son's killers,
didn't seem to want the liability of the murderous couple and
had expelled them from their fold.

The rage beneath the Shepherd's somber tone was uncompromising. Why he'd be so upset about the death of a woman
not of his blood was nonsensical. Delilah was a tool, yet the
Shepherd carried on as if she would ascend the throne of
power his son would have.

Max took a sip of his drink.

Duval Andrews was obviously losing himself to this role
he'd created, but Max knew the man before he had a flock or
a keep. Over twenty years was apparently the length of time it
took a *reformed* dredge to be poisoned by the ideological
Kool-Aid he served others.

"I understand your pain my friend," Max said solemnly.
"And I grieve with you."

Max wanted to point out that it was the Shepherd's own
decision to send Delilah on the hunt for his son's killer. Max
had never even liked the chit, but in this time of limited
support, he held his tongue. Maintaining alliances was crucial
right now.

There was no, *it's God's will*, response. Instead, the Good Shepherd spoke of vengeance.

Max rolled his eyes and took another sip of whiskey. It appeared good old Duval was high off his own supply...the blood of Christ or some such thing.

"Delilah was a special woman," Max interrupted, hoping to rush the other man off the phone. "Like my son, Delilah was a beloved child. I stand on the precipice of vengeance for us both and this time there will be no failure."

"And what will you do?" the Shepherd asked after an extended silence.

"I'll do nothing but wait for Basir's assassin to destroy them. Delilah's final report proves the couple were a part of Cornelius' death, and even if they weren't responsible for Delilah's, it stands to reason that they'd know who murdered her. Once I find out who killed Delilah, I'll let you know. This will be my gift to you."

"Tell me where you are. I'll send six Brothers of the order to meet you. *They* will bring Zeus and Sabrina here, where they will be broken, purged, and delivered to hell."

The idea had merit, but there was the issue of the child. Max didn't trust that the Good Shephard wouldn't steal her away. It's what his order was built on. Max's child would not become a new addition to the Shepherd's flock. She would not be taking Delilah's place in Duval's affections.

"Don't worry," Max said, reassuringly. "I've just met with Basir's man here in Paris and it's been arranged. He'll arrive in Marseille sometime tomorrow, dispose of my son's killer and my son's whore and will... Again, my thanks to Delilah for delivering this information, for bringing my son's recently discovered child to my awareness. The child is not a replacement for Max, but she is blood; my wife wants her in our care."

The Good Shepherd didn't respond immediately.

Max feared that Duval would try to divest himself of the Consortium altogether, after hearing about Delilah's death. The order was now the only faction that procured and groomed the ones that served the appetites of the Consortium's membership. Really, with all these scandals the entertainment the Shephard's Keep provided was one of the few joys they had left.

He realized he could not lose the Shepherd's support now.

"If the Brothers are more skilled than Basir's assassin and can take Zeus and the woman," he relented, "they have my support. You can sacrifice the two at the shrine of Delilah for all I care; I just want my grandchild."

"My men will work with or against Basir's heathen. It simply depends on whether he attempts to interfere in my righteous justice."

Max hadn't visited the Shephard's Keep in years, but there had been a time when Duval played a role. Now there was a darkness that practically seeped through the phone. Perhaps Delilah's death had truly destroyed his sanity.

"Understood," Maxim stated. "Have the Brothers come to my yacht tomorrow evening. I'll give them the same information I provided to Basir's man."

Maxim disconnected the call.

In the span of an hour, he'd gone from having one person hunting Zeus and Sabrina to seven. With those numbers, the murderous pair would be dead in a matter of days.

~

Zeus opened his eyes, awake instantly.

The sound of feet moving stealthily towards the bedroom didn't cause concern; instead, he slipped his hand beneath the pillow under his head and slid the large blade free.

A dark silhouette appeared in the center of the doorway, watching without advancing.

"Close the door," he ordered, twisting his blade languidly. He didn't know the exact time, but he was the only one in the bed. That needed to change.

The figure stepped through the door and closed it.

"Everything is quiet."

Her voice was just above a whisper, reaching for him through the dark. "You're rested," she said, stripping. "*We're* rested."

He hummed in satisfaction when she locked the door.

"Stop moving." He rose up and rounded the foot of the bed, knife clutched against his side, ready. He reached for her throat, gripped it, stroked his thumb across the side of her neck before lowering his head, kissing her as he eased his blade up from the base of her t-shirt, slicing up the center, sparing only her bra. She didn't like when he cut her clothes off, but she let him tonight. He deserved whatever he wanted because –

"I've been good this whole trip. No violence–"

"The man at the airport?"

"Fucker's still alive." He gently bit the side of her neck, sucked, bit again, pressing her against the door and widening his legs. "No knives around Bri," he added.

She gripped his hand that held the blade, feeling him slowly cut the material from her hip to her thigh on the left, and repeated the motion on the right, hip to thigh, until her panties and bed shorts lay in pieces at their feet.

Sabrina's thumb rubbed the woven hilt of his blade and he chuffed out a burst of air as arousal tightened the skin surrounding his ball-sack, engorging his already thick erection.

"You have been good," she whispered, wrapping her free hand around the back of his neck. He did not loosen his grip on the front of hers. "No," she clarified. "You've haven't been good, you've been perfect."

She pulled his head down low enough that their breathes rebounded against their still untouching lips. "The most generous, loving, perfect man I've ever known."

"That's because before me, your taste in men was shit," he reminded. It was the truth.

She laughed instead of being upset.

"It was, until you."

Even *with* him. But he wasn't telling her that. He wasn't gonna be the one to give her a reason to leave him.

Sabrina pulled his fingers from around her throat and maneuvered him back, pushing him onto the bed. He shed his clothing while lying down, settled his head on the pillow, and watched as she unhooked her bra and tossed it to the side. Crawling up the bed, she crept over him, until her breasts dangled above his head and her sex, sweet and musky, ripe for eating and fucking, suspended just over his overflowing erection.

He slid his blade beneath the pillow, shielding it from their raw appetites.

She stood on her knees, towering above him, gripped each of his hands and brought them to her breasts, molding them to her, guiding them in a leisurely stroke and massage. He added his own squeeze and nipple pinch and she groaned in pleasure.

Zeus sat up with her in his lap, and they touched chest to breast. He allowed her to lead his motions. Until it wasn't enough.

He didn't want her soft sighs, he wanted to hear her scream, hear her beg. It had been so long, too long, and he deserved.

Exchanging one breast for one globe of her ass, he pressed her tight against his erection, just the feel of her slickness. He was torn because he hadn't tasted her, he needed to taste her, her heat, but he cupped her breast instead, held it high as he wrapped his mouth around her nipple, sucking fast, hard, hard enough that as much breast filled his mouth as nipple.

Sabrina wrapped her palm over her mouth and screamed into it as she ground and gyrated against his dick.

He gripped her hair and she cried out in surprise as he bowed her backwards making her breasts an offering, her body a platter he feasted from, and he ate, and sucked, and bit into, until it wasn't enough.

"Until you," she panted out, over and over, chanting.

Until *him*.

In one fluid motion he put her on her back and drove into her hard, deep, through her muffled screams and grunts, through the pleasure that only got sharper and sharper until it pierced through his spine, his head, his heart, and his seed shot from him, racing to fill her, racing to find its resting place in her because she was home, she was earth, she was an complicated sort of peace that he'd never allowed himself to have. Until her.

His body calmed, cooled, but he stayed on top of her, becoming more attuned to the sounds and scents and textures around him.

Sabrina wrapped her legs around his hips, feet resting

against his ass as she stroked his hair, kissed the crown of his head.

"I missed you Big Man," she sighed. "I missed this."

"It's because I have the fucking skills of a God. Makes sense you would."

"You're an idiot," she laughed.

He was far from it. But for her he would be pretend.

"I'm good with kids," he reflected, after a few minutes of her caresses.

"You're good with *Bri*."

He adjusted her breasts to cushion his head the way he liked. "I'm good at fathering."

"It's galling," she mumbled. "You slipped into this whole new parent thing so easily. I feel like I'm stumbling with every other step."

"It's 'cause—"

Her hand stilled.

"You *bet* not say something about *stupid woman brain chatter*."

He rubbed his nose against her nipple to distract from the fact that that's exactly what he was going to say.

Sabrina laughed again. "I can practically *hear* you thinking it, you're not fooling me," she said tugging at a lock of hair.

He smiled into her breast. They could practically communicate telepathically now. Was that a part of loving someone?

"I was going to say it because it's true," he informed her. "Sorry if you can't handle it."

She tried to wrestle him off her, but he'd waited too long to be in this exact position. He wasn't budging.

He let her flop around beneath him until she had the sense to give up.

Then her arms wrapped around his shoulders, and she held him tightly to her.

"Man, this is *crazy*." He heard the tears in her voice and looked up. "How can I love you so much?"

He pulled away and gazed down at her, able to see her clearly through the shadows. This trip had made her more emotional, more anxious, he knew. She was trying too hard to do things the right way but wasn't sure what the right way was.

"Didn't believe love existed," he said, nuzzling her neck. "Then..." He eased his hand between their bodies dipping his fingers into her hot gushy center. "You."

She sucked in a hissing breath as if burned. "Then us."

He removed his fingers and fed her with his dick. She moaned and arched.

His glide was slow. Slow in, slow out.

Even when his finger circled her clit fast, faster, stroked it, her, into another moaning orgasm. But him, he took his time. He liked to play with his prey when he had the time, and she... she was his prey tonight. He preyed on her love, fucking so deep he was sure he'd planted another womb full of his seed, and what fruit they bore only the Blade Spirits knew.

He and Sabrina dozed, they fucked, talked, they planned. This was the ritual he'd craved. Missed. And when it was completed, they finally slept.

~

Sabrina woke to an empty bed, an empty room.

She stretched wide, smiling, and made a bed angel.

That man made her happy. He was the only man she'd

willingly shared every part of herself with because she knew he could hold them all. The good and the not so good.

She sent a prayer of gratitude to her mother and sister; certain they were blessing her from whatever point of heaven they watched down from, then hopped out of bed with renewed energy, promptly falling to her ass. She gripped her mouth to staunch the urge to vomit because the room spun, literally went topsy turvy, and the room dimmed and blurred before coming back into focus.

No. Just no, she told her body, because if it was telling her what she thought it was telling her, she wasn't ready.

Girl you better get ready, she practically heard her mother.

There was a commotion on the other side of the bedroom door, and she heard *him*. That fucking man. That fucking man and his fucking demon sperm that just couldn't wait until they'd settled into their new life. No patience. Just like its donor.

Resting her head on the side of the bed, she took deep breaths and eventually the urge to throw up receded, but the nausea remained. She could deal with nausea. *You can deal with nausea*, she thought again, encouraging herself.

She stood slowly, sinking down onto the bed.

She wasn't ready to be a mother; she was just learning how to be a decent aunt!

Fuck.

That's what you *get*, the old bitter voice in her head taunted, *did you think* love *was a prophylactic*? No. She truly didn't believe she could get pregnant. In all these years, nothing. Not even when her ex, Ernesto, tried his damnedest, hoping it would tie her to him for life.

The thought of having a baby.... Briana was fine, she could take care of herself in a lot of ways, but a baby.

Stop, just stop, she thought, feeling herself spiraling. She didn't even know if she was really pregnant.

But she *knew*.

Burying her face in covers that smelled of fucking baby making activities, she teared up. Her mother and sister weren't alive to experience all these moments with her. Her mother was probably side eyeing her and laughing because Sabrina had vowed as a child, that she was never having kids. And Sam...Sam would be so excited. Even in her low moments, she was always happy when good things came Sabrina's way.

And this maybe-baby, it was a good thing. Not the best timing but it was made of nothing but love. It would be a part of her mother, and her sister that lived on, just like Bri. Also, just like Bri, it would have a not quite right father, plus his Blade Spirits and his family they would soon meet.

Wiping her face, she stood and went to the dresser across from the bed and dug through the top and middle drawers for clothes and underwear. Opening the door, she slowly made her way across the hall to the bathroom, slipping inside and locking it before she had to face Zeus or Briana.

Showered and dressed, she put her twists into a top bun and stared at herself in the mirror. Outside of red and slightly swollen eyes, there wasn't a hint of the turmoil she'd experienced through a few minutes ago.

Shit, she and Zeus were going to be parents.

She cut off a bark of laughter.

He might have his freaking Godzuki after all.

Running cold water over her face towel she folded it and leaned back, placing the towel over her eyes to reduce the puffiness. She decided then and there that she wasn't going to say anything about being pregnant until she knew for sure.

It would be better for everybody if she was sure.

Briana was dealing with her grief and a major transition, and Zeus... she shook her head. "You poor kid."

Walking out of the bathroom she headed down the wide hall towards the kitchen. The smell of pancakes and bacon caused the Kaiju seed inside of her to growl in discontent.

"You two are a menace," she said as she stepped into the kitchen. "You really would've just let me sleep and ate all the food yourselves, wouldn't you?" she asked, placing a kiss on Briana's cheek.

The child never stopped chomping on her bacon, but at least she nodded. Kids were ruthless. Zeus squinted at her but continued putting food onto a plate he slid across the butcher-block island towards her. He didn't say anything. No good morning, no I love you, no you look beautiful this morning. He simply watched her as if she were a curiosity.

"I'm *starving*", she said dramatically, trying to ease her apprehension. Something had happened while she slept. She could tell by that watchful stillness he had even when in motion.

She glanced at Bri, knowing she couldn't ask the questions she wanted to ask until curious ears weren't listening.

"How was your first night sleeping in an actual French bed?"

Bri never stopped eating, just nodded, and twinkled her fingers in the air.

"I'm... gonna assume that means magical?"

Bri laughed. Kid never stopped eating.

Sabrina frowned at her, sure that this was some new anti-verbal habit she was picking up from Zeus.

"Lord help," Sabrina whispered, reaching for her food.

She actually moaned in pleasure as bit into the thick slice of bacon.

This had to be some non-GMO, organic, plant fed, happy French countryside pig for this bacon to be so damn delicious. She ate two slices in under thirty seconds. And her body punished her for it. She began dry heaving, stumbled off the bar stool and fell on her ass again as she pressed her arm into her stomach.

"Don't die, please don't die," Bri cried as she lunged out of her seat and threw herself against Sabina on the ground, hugging her desperately. The terror on the child's face reminded Sabrina that beneath all the smiles and charm, Bri had just lost the only father figure she'd known and was thousands of miles away from the mother figure who'd nurtured and raised her.

Sabrina held Bri close and stroking her wild curls as she rocked, the motion soothing her stomach as much as it soothed Briana.

Zeus, on the other hand, wasn't fazed. He went to the refrigerator, poured a glass of sparkling water, and handed it to her.

"Drink."

She drank.

He walked away, disappearing into the panty across the hall from the kitchen. Sabrina pulled Bri into her lap, resting her head against her shoulder feeling awkward but knowing that this was something a good mother would do.

"It's okay, I'm not dying, I promise you," she assured, though she was sure this might feel worse.

Zeus returned and she squinted to see what he held pinched between his fingers as he squatted down and placed the church wafer sized slice of ginger root to her mouth.

"Open."

She opened her mouth.

"Chew."

She did as ordered, and after a few seconds her stomach settled.

Zeus sat in Briana's chair and stared down at Sabrina.

There was humor in his eyes. And knowing.

He was such a smug bastard.

"Say it."

"I won't," she glared.

"Say what?" Bri asked, lifting her head.

Zeus smiled. A smile with no shadows, no darkness, just sheer fucking audacity and satisfaction. *Lord, if that man smiles like this on a regular basis, I'm gonna have to give him a spawn of kids just to keep seeing it.*

It didn't survive long. But for a moment it existed.

"He wants me to say he's a God," Sabrina told Bri.

"Mrs. Jace would tell him not to blaspheme."

"And she would be right."

"Say it," Zeus repeated. He was like a fucking pitbull locked on her throat.

She ground the ginger beneath her molars and glared at him. "You realize Kaijus are monsters right," she emphasized for clarification.

"Yes. That can destroy worlds. Say it."

"I'm so lost," Briana whispered, looking from Sabrina to Zeus.

"She's going to have my baby and we're going to call him Godzuki; now I want her to acknowledge who I am." So much for keeping this all a secret.

"We're not calling the kid Godzuki."

"Say it."

She laughed against Bri's temple. "Man, I'm not saying that!"

Zeus leaned forward clasping his hand between his spread knees as he tilted his head and watched her patiently.

This was some bullshit.

"You are Zeus," she stated in monotone. "My Algerian-Greek God,"

"If he's a God, what does that make you?" Bri asked.

"Sorely put upon."

"The mother of world destroyers," Zeus corrected.

Yeah, that's exactly how she wanted to be known.

"And me?" Bri asked.

"The child of two extremely odd people?" Sabrina offered.

"She's odd. I'm a God. And you're the caterpillar inside the cocoon, still waiting to spread your spirit wings. We'll know your name then."

"And when I have my name, then you really *really* can't give me up?"

"Little girl, let me tell you something," Sabrina snapped in anger and fear. "When I was in foster care as a kid, I did *the most* to get kicked out of my foster homes. I always succeeded in getting sent back to my mother. Always. So, if this is some roundabout way of saying you want to go back to Mrs. Jace's instead of staying with us, trust, you are *doomed* because you messed up and got us as new parents. So, if we live around *truly* unstable, but good people, guess what, you're living around unstable people. If we live in a treehouse on the highest mountain in the world, you better get used to goddamn heights because you'll be living there too, you hear me. If I have to tie you up and carry you over my shoulder—"

"I would cut you free," Zeus said.

"Shut it!" she snapped, refocusing on Bri. "If I have to

carry you over my shoulder to keep you with us, that's how it's going to be. In a few months you'll *possibly* be a big sister, so if I gotta live with bringing a whole *human* life into our family, you'll be right there holding my hand, so don't play with me."

Bri began to cry and Sabrina, holding her tight, began to cry too and she didn't know why. It would be super irresponsible to not let Bri go if they weren't the best for her, but she just didn't believe she could.

"It just feels so *good*," Briana hickuped. "Like I'm where I'm supposed to be. I would just *die* if I ever had to leave you guys."

"Oh my God you are so much drama!" Sabrina laughed, whipping her tears with unsteady fingers.

"I *am*" Bri smiled, whipping her tears on her pajama sleeve. "Didn't you see me in *Annie* last month?"

Zeus hadn't moved from his position during the whole exchange, but his fingers danced in a pattern she'd never seen.

"You got something to say Big Man?"

He pulled Bri into his lap and lifted her hand, examined it front to back, finger by finger, adjusted her hand into a fist and pressed it against his palm and pushed so she was forced to push it back.

He nodded.

"Get dressed," he told Briana. "It's time to learn control and balance. The Blade Spirits say it's time for them to train you."

Sabrina wasn't going to object to Bri's training, but it was late in the morning and they were on a timeline.

"We should probably get to Marseille earlier than later. Give you and your family time to get to know each other."

He nodded in the direction of the ceiling and Bri hopped

off his lap and skittered on swift feet towards the front of the house and up the stairs.

"And don't forget to brush your teeth and wash your face!" Sabrina called out.

"What am I a barbarian?" Bri yelled down. "I always brush my teeth and wash my face. *And* make my bed."

"Oh no she didn't," Sabrina muttered, rising with Zeus's help.

He pulled her against him, and she wrapped her arms around his waist. His face was stern as he looked down at her, but she knew he was laughing on the inside. His eyes were always the tell.

"She's a wise and honest child. You should just make the bed."

"I won't! And I will not be shamed into it."

She was way too stubborn for that.

"Terry called while you were asleep. Delilah's dead," he said in his abrupt way. "Kragen-the-father went to Mrs. Jace's house. Son of a bitch definitely knows about Brianna."

He must've expected her knees to go weak because he held her tight as he gave her the information. If Kragen knew about Bri, would he try to take her away from them? They had to run −

"Stop," Zeus said. "We knew this would happen eventually. If he finds us, he'll find himself leaving without Bri. If he won't go willingly, he won't go at all. There's an area in the yard I can bury him, and no one will ever find him. It'll be his choice. Now," he guided her back to the small island. "Eat, stay healthy, our Kaiju will need your strength." He walked towards the pantry, but instead of opening the door on the left he pushed an area of the wall opposite wall, moving it inward.

Of course, he would have a hidden room, she thought and reached for an apple.

"I'll take Bri for a couple of hours, accelerate her self-defense training," Zeus said from inside the hidden space. "If one of the blades chooses her, she'll also get her own Spirit Blade and begin training with it.

"Those are my priorities. My biological family doesn't even know I exist, so I meet them on my own time. That's means after Bri's lesson and after you've eaten and rested. This family comes first, so call Mama, and Randy, and Stormy and whoever else you gossip with, and tell them the child of Zeus will soon be entering this physical realm."

"I'll just tell them we *may* be pregnant. And I don't gossip."

Zeus brow was arched in judgement when he walked back through the wall and closed it. The brow stayed that way as he passed her on the way to the backyard.

Reaching for her plate, she took it to the microwave acknowledging that just because she'd found love in this man, found family with Bri, it didn't mean the world would miraculously grant her everlasting peace. Kragen the father was a threat, and she needed her family prepared to face it, which was why she quietly ate her food as Bri steaked through the kitchen to the back yard to train.

CHAPTER FIVE

"This place is spooky," Brianna whispered, as they entered St. Catherine's church. The church, one of three buildings on the campus, was in ill repair. It was the only building accessible to the public. The dorms that the nuns and children had shared and the hospital, St. Catherine's Hôpital Pour Les Indigents, had been shuttered long ago.

The two-story dorm was southwest of the church, and the hospital, where he was born, was almost south and slightly east of the church. Each building formed a trinity, crowding the courtyard where children once played.

An unholy trinity, Zeus thought, shifting as a disheveled old man shuffled through the front doors of the church, and down the main aisle. This place was more of a blight, patroned by graffiti artists, the occasional drug dealer, and on rare occasions, those bold enough to step on the grounds for an illicit triste. Most thought the campus was haunted and avoided it.

This was his first home. And he'd survived it. And despite

everything, there had been laughter here before it was shut down, now only the broken-down church was in use, an act of penance if you asked him. The children that fueled this places existence were long gone, but many hadn't made it off the grounds alive.

He was one of the lucky ones, and came here every time he returned to Marseille to remind himself of that, to remind the church that their shit wasn't forgotten and to visit with the spirits of the ones who remained.

"Place was spooky even when it was supposed to be the beacon of supposed charity and good works," he muttered, walking slowly down the aisle to inspect the shadowy parishioners. "Shit was false as fu–"

"Zeus," Sabrina interrupted harshly.

Yeah, kid ears.

He looked down to see said kid watching him with judgmental eyes.

"You can't curse in church," Briana reminded him.

Church still meant good for her. It was the years with the Jaces, he knew.

"I can," he clarified. "*You* can't."

"Why is that little boy looking at you like that?" Sabrina asked, strangely.

Zeus gazed over at her. "Real or ghost?"

"Lord, please let him be real," she said, motioning to the back of the church. In the large arched opening of the wall to the left, a brown skinned boy with an afro made of large wild curls squatted, partially hidden behind the wall.

"Real," Zeus said, moving towards him.

The moment the boy realized he was the focus of Zeus's attention; he ran down the hall in the direction of the back door. Zeus heard it push open and slam shut moments before he entered the hall. Pulling the blade at his back, he advanced slowly down the back hall, pausing to see Sabrina and Bri behind him but at a healthy distance. Sabrina's arm extended back as she kept Bri held behind her, tucked against her side and the wall.

Zeus felt proud because Bri held her newly gifted blade in her hand. Ready. *Kid's a natural*, he smiled as he walked through the door. Unlike her aunt, Bri took to the blade as if was born into her hand.

He grunted as a thought hit him. He needed to make Godzuki a blade. It would be his Christening gift.

"Vous avez du travail pour moi?" The boy asked pensively, standing before the backdrop of the broken metal swing structure lying on the ground as if it had been frozen in time while attempting to crawl away to its death. A domed jungle gym, brown with rust stood defiant to the left of the collapsed swings, as if protecting unseen spirits inside. It had a purpose.

Zeus looked the boy up and down. Jean-Pierre was eleven now, still skinny but he'd grown at least four inches since last year. Kid had been clear about his purpose since he was six – to help his family of five live. He'd did it by evading tourists he'd picked clean after their dollar to euro currency exchange. Kid learned quick that Zeus wasn't a tourist, quicker that he couldn't be evaded.

Zeus pulled three hundred euros from his wallet and held it out. "Down payment," he said. "Got family business."

"D'accord," JP said, taking the money. "Bonjour, famille de l'homme Dieu," JP said, shyly to Sabrina and Bri.

Zeus turned to smirk at Sabrina.

"I don't care who says it and how many times, and in what language, you're not a God. Bonjour," she softly to Jean-Pierre. *Why didn't I get the same softness*, Zeus wondered?

"He said man-god," Bri clarified, and twinkled her fingers at JP. "Bonjour. Je m'appelle Bri, et... et elle est, Sabrina."

Zeus frowned when JP's smile widened. It disappeared the moment he saw Zeus's scowl.

"Call me when you need, ouias?" JP said.

Zeus nodded once and watched the boy leave through a break in the fence bordering the courtyard.

"Why did you give him money?" Briana asked, as they continued towards the dorms.

"He does odd jobs for me when I visit. Helps his family."

"You're just a big old softy," Sabrina bumped his shoulder.

He stopped, pressed his lips to her ear and whispered. "Where?"

Her breath hitched as if his voice touched her deep inside.

"Come on," Zeus smirked.

Within the hour he showed them the places he slept, fought, bled. Took them to a place in one of the isolation chambers where he'd buried a mask. In all these years he'd never thought about it until now. Removing a stone from the wall and digging into the soil his fingers touched on what he'd been looking for. After all these years was still here. He pulled it out and dusted it off.

"You're like a freaking squirrel, always hiding stuff in secret places."

"Not hiding, giving them a place to rest until they're needed." He shrugged and looked up at her. "And I don't like losing what's mine."

"No," she said. "You really don't."

"What is it?" Bri asked, bending down beside him to get a better view.

"Picked it from a store when I was little." When he said picked up, he meant stole, but per Sabrina, he had to factor in kid ears. "If the nuns and priests could call me the devil, I wanted to conjure up what they kept calling forth." Things had changed not long after that, and they only called him by his name. The name of a God.

Zeus placed the red half-mask over his eyes.

It was small now, but as a kid the devil mask – with its dramatically arched black eyebrows and small curved horns painted on each side – covered most of his face.

Two small arms wrapped around his neck.

"I'm sorry they were mean to you Big Man. You didn't deserve for them to be mean to you. I hope your mask scared them. Can we go meet your family now? They'll treat you better, I know it."

He stood, lifting her in his arms.

He didn't know it.

But the sooner this reunion was done, the sooner he could get back to his new family. Hell, he had a whole Godzuki to bond with. He looked over at Sabrina standing in the rubble of his childhood with the fierceness of an avenging angel. One that loved him, one that would've likely bitch-slapped the nuns and priests for how they treated him if they were there today.

He pulled her to him as they made their way out of the dorms.

"So...should I call you Big Man, or" she touched the mask dangling from his fingers. "Should I call you Devil-man?" Her eyes danced. He leveled her with a flat look. Responding verbally would only encourage her.

They stepped outside, and the warmth of the Mediterranean sun immediately washed over them, cleansing the toxic energy of this place. Walking away, Zeus determined that he'd come back here one last time before they left

France, complete a final ritual laying to rest whatever spirits wanted to be free of this place. But once he was gone, he wouldn't come back. This was his past, now he had more reason to shift his energy to the present and the future.

Climbing out of the SUV, they bunched together on the sidewalk looking up at the four-story building. This part of the city was very bourgeoise, distant from the city center but still had a lot of foot traffic.

Unwilling to put a lot of distance between him, Briana, and Sabrina, Zeus scanned the area instead of searching for threats. Plus, he had enough variations of bladed weapons on him to throw, slice, fillet, or chop through flesh and bone with one concentrated use of force. For now, they were good.

He and Sabrina had looked over the schematics of the building Terry'd provided before they'd left Mama's House. His mother lived in a three-bedroom flat on the fourth floor. If he was here alone, he'd have been in and out; only the ones he wanted to see him would've seen him. Now days, one of the only things he did alone was hunt.

"Maybe we should've called ahead." Sabrina sounded uncertain. "This is a lot to just spring on somebody don't you think? Maybe she's not even here..."

She was doing it again, just like when she sat in the car in front of the Jaces'.

"Why am I so anxious? These aren't even my people," she muttered.

She was anxious because she wanted him to be accepted. She shouldn't.

"She's up there," Zeus assured. He felt it.

"But let's be clear, I'm here for you. You want me to care about these people, but I don't."

"I just want them to know you exist, at least give them the opportunity to love you as much as we do. And even if *you* don't care, I will be *pissed* if they hurt you."

She didn't get it.

He truly didn't give a shit. He had more in this life than he'd believed possible. "There's nothing in blood I haven't seen before." He'd spilled vats of blood over the years and was therefore assured that even if he cut the flesh of the woman who'd given him to the orphanage, he wouldn't find anything to tie her to him nearly as strong as the bond he had with Sabrina and Bri.

"You're probably right." He was absolutely right. "I'm putting too much on this. As long as we have each other."

"All I've been saying."

Zeus buzzed the buildings gated door and waited. The intercom clicked on.

"Mon fils, mon couer, where have you been? I've been waiting for you forever, non?"

Zeus looked at Sabrina questioningly. She shrugged in confusion.

The door buzzed and they walked into a large marble foyer, decorated with ornate wallpaper and trim. To the left was a curved stairway, a black gated elevator was straight ahead, and to the right, an opening that led to a cobble stoned courtyard with access for the residents use only. Two children laughed and rode bikes out there, playing a two wheeled version of tag. They stopped to stare at them as they walk towards the elevator, but their gazes lingered on Bri.

She reached for his hand as she looked out at the children.

He couldn't protect her from whatever she was feeling,

but he picked her up anyway. She was capable of standing and walking on her own two feet, but if they said something cruel, having her in his arms would stop him from pulling his blades.

As they entered the elevator, Bri asked: "Why did that woman say she's been waiting for you forever? Does she think you're the UPS guy?"

"She said *my son, my heart.*"

"Maybe it was too much to expect Mama not to interfere," Sabrina said.

Mama was the most interfering person in creation, so yeah, maybe it was too much.

Zeus pulled the thin silver chain with the small ring looped through it from around his neck and held both in his fist. The elevator stopped and he lowered Bri to the ground, drawing the accordion gate back.

"If this goes tits up, we give her the ring and bounce?" Sabrina said under her breath, as they walked down the hallway, stopping at the flat he knew his biological mother owned.

Zeus's rumbling laughter vibrated against the door, seemed to push it open, because when he recovered from the unexpected burst of humor Sabrina caused, he saw a little assed woman who barely cleared chest, standing there, her long wavy black and gray - mostly gray - hair fell to her shoulder blades. She had dove gray eyes.

He frowned and looked back at Sabrina for confirmation that the woman wasn't a figment of his imagination.

Her nod was almost imperceptible, but he saw it, knew that the woman who stood looking up at him was probably a relative, maybe his mother, but he felt no connection, no recognition. He should feel that shouldn't he? Like animal instinct, mother and child instantly recognizing each other by scent alone?

She stared at him, waiting, like she was owed something, and his frown turned into a glare.

"Please stop growling," Sabrina whispered. He went silent, looked past the woman to the flat beyond, decorated in deep reds, golds, and cream. It was elegant space, like the woman still silently guarding the entrance. Zeus heard a man and another woman's voice coming from the left, could smell food, something creamy and rich with herbs. Bread... he tilted his head fennel and garlic.

The woman's hand went to her neck, and she clutched it as if holding back her words.

He extended the chain and ring and she reached for it with a trembling hand. She gripped the necklace and examined the ring closely, her eyes flew back to his, searching, then she backed up, looked at the ring closer, shaking her head.

Falling to her knees, she screamed, clutching the ring against her breast as if it was the infant son she'd abandoned decades ago.

It was her.

He knew because only someone who'd left their infant son could wail with such shame. Had to be her.

A thin man, older, fairer skinned, maybe Greek, not much larger than the woman, dashed into the room moving swiftly to her as she curled nearly into a ball, head touching her knees as she rocked and wailed.

Bri pressed her face against his waist, her warm tears seeping through his shirt.

"What is it, Zahira, what's wrong?" The slightly balding man asked in French, trying to be heard over the woman. He was so distracted by her pained cries that he didn't notice the three of them on the other side of the door.

Sabrina rested a hand on Bri's head, while the other

rubbed up and down Zeus's back. He wasn't the one who needed comfort, it was the French woman who seemed to have the emotional restraint of a colicky chihuahua.

Another woman, mid-seventies to early eighties, scuttled into the room, brushing her hands on her apron, asking the couple on the floor what was wrong.

"Je ne sais pas!" The man shouted, trying to uncurl the screaming woman.

Zeus sighed heavily and looked over at Sabrina.

There was a reason he preferred beginning his blade's dance against an opponent's throat, it spared his ears from the screaming, the begging, the undignified noise of humanity resisting the pull of death.

Zeus's fingers danced against the back of Bri's neck.

He didn't want to kill the woman, but he wanted the anguished sounds she made to end. The way she was going on and on you'd think he'd actually put a shiv through her heart, as if he were killing her. As if his very presence was her undoing.

She was the one who'd abandoned him, but he wasn't losing his shit.

The tears Sabrina and Bri shed when they met was understandable, they had love and the shared bond of Samantha which had only grown in the time they'd gone from video and phone contact to coming face to face. This shit.... he didn't have the patience. It was time to go.

"You! What have you done, eh? What have you done to my child?" the old woman gestured at him, kneeling to pull the woman into her arms, quieting her where the man could not. Thank fucking god for that.

"Appelez la police!" the old woman ordered the man.

Zeus cocked a brow and flattened Sabrina with a look.

"Now can we take Bri to swim in the sea. We can even go back to town, have dinner at Salino's a half-mile from the house. You'll both like it. Pizza and Spaghetti, better than that shit in America."

"No!"

The woman fought to free herself and rushed over to them, hugging Zeus around the waist with Bri caught in the woman's embrace. Bri looked at him with wide eyes, silently asking what she should do.

"Shit if I know kid," he said, holding his arms out wide, not comfortable with touching the woman in return.

"I don't like to be touched," he warned Sabrina. Only she and Bri had the right.

The older woman was shouting at the man in Arabic. Zeus didn't know the language fluently, could only make out a few words but knew she was going on about police and criminals and –

"Arrez!" the woman holding him shouted, pulling away.

"On ten," Zeus told Sabrina. Meaning in ten seconds he was walking the fuck out of here and not looking back.

Sabrina stepped around him and Bri.

"I'm sorry, parles-tu Anglais?"

"Oui, oui oui," the woman said to Sabina, wiping her face. "Je parle Anglaise. I speak English!" she revised.

"My name is Sabrina, this is Bri, and this is, we believe, your–"

"My son, yes."

She pressed her hand against Zeus's chest. He slowly lifted his hand to remove it, but Bri caught it and held it with both of hers.

He glared down at her.

"Mon fil," the woman said again.

"Just Zeus," he said.

"Oui," she smiled. "Like the God. Come, Come," she said, pulling him into the home.

"Maman, you said if it were God's will, my son would return to me, yes? God has willed it."

Zeus looked at the older woman.

She had light gray eyes like her daughter and though she was thinner, she seemed less fragile. She stared at him, and he could see dawning acceptance in her gaze.

"This is my husband, Victor," the woman said.

Victor was shorter than Sabrina, but his wife was literally only a few inches taller than Bri, so they made sense. Victor looked fit for his age, but nowhere near as fit as Terry. And Mama, Mama would break all three of them in minutes.

"Bonjour," Victor smiled. "It is nice to meet you."

The man was French, not Algerian or Greek, and she'd said her husband, not your father. Victor's smile was welcoming but anxious, as if the woman had just led a dangerous animal into their home.

Which she has, Zeus half-smiled.

He looked at the family. He'd now met the woman who'd given him away, and knew he had a living grandmother named Nabeela.

Was there something else he was supposed to say?

He wouldn't.

Was there something else he was supposed to feel?

He didn't.

He turned to Sabrina.

"You ready?"

"Um... don't you want to–"

"Nah."

"No, no, you must stay," the woman plead, reaching for his

free hand, which he moved behind him, resting it on the hilt of the blade at his back.

"Taking the kid to the water before it gets too late."

Why was he explaining himself? Then he remembered the woman's earlier display of emotion and knew that he didn't want experience it again.

"You have your ring back; you know I exist," he looked at Sabrina. "That's what we said we were here to do."

"Maybe you come back tonight, for dinner yes, meet more family," the woman begged him.

"That would be wonderful," Sabrina replied.

He frowned at her and she threw him a look that said Do. Not.

He grunted, pulled his lip back in a silent sneer, then settled cold eyes on the woman.

"What time?"

"Huit heures, it's okay?"

He nodded and moved to the door, needing to get free of this fucking place. He'd stayed too long, the walls, the expectations, were beginning to feel like a cage, wild things didn't do good in cages.

Bri waved goodbye as Sabrina opened the door and walked through it, jumping out of the way so he could shut it firmly behind them.

They made their way towards the elevator.

"That was weird as shit," Zeus said.

"Maybe tonight will be better," Sabrina offered.

"I met her; I don't know what more you're looking for."

"I don't know, I just feel there's power in knowing, Zeus, - the full story of you, the story *before* you. For good or bad."

She closed her eyes and rubbed her temple.

She'd thrown up twice before they left the house. Maybe

she needed to rest, maybe Godzuki was pulling too much energy from her. He should take her home, but he knew it would be a battle. It was her brain. It got stuck in stubbornness, like a small knife lodged in a large bone. It wasn't moving without fucking up everything around it. And he wasn't down for more fucking drama.

Pressing the elevator's call button, he pulled her backwards into his chest and kissed her temple. She sighed. He felt her body relax against his.

"You might not feel a bond with your family, and you don't have to," she said. "But I don't know, I just feel there's something in knowing. If you don't want to come back, we don't have to."

That was the difference between them. What was important to him was now, the future. She focused on now and what had been, but life was what you made of it, not who you were made from.

Thinking about Godzuki though, he would want his child to know his story, would want to share how he was shaped and tempered by his experiences just like he'd shared them with Sabrina and Bri today. The man he was today was greater than the man he'd been before Sabrina, and the father he would be with Godzuki and Bri would make him greater still. He looked at Sabrina. He would make her believe in his God status yet.

The elevator arrived and Zeus opened it. A man stepped out, dismissing Zeus and Bri immediately, his only interest was Sabrina.

Made sense; she was enticing.

The blade was in his palm, twirling through his fingers at a rate that drew everyone's attention. Zeus kept his gaze trained on the man. Fucker's eyes widened, now they watched him unwaveringly, fearfully.

The man cleared his throat and looked down as he stepped out of the elevator and made his way down the hall glancing back, probably to make sure he wasn't being pursued. Zeus snorted. Message received without the need for bloodshed.

They stepped inside the elevator and the blade went back into its resting state.

"I thought we agreed no blades in front of Bri unless absolutely necessary."

He looked from Sabrina to Bri.

"It was necessary," he said closing the gate. "Why?" he asked Briana.

"The blade saved his life instead of taking it. It was a warning," she told Sabrina. "The guy was smart enough to get that he shouldn't have looked at you like you didn't have a man *right here*." She swept her little hand up and down the length of Zeus.

"Kid learns *so* much faster than you," Zeus said. "That's why you train them young."

Sabrina looked to the heavens. "I don't know how I'm gonna manage with you two, I just really don't."

"You'll find a way," Zeus said.

He believed in her.

Aahod brought the sleek black sedan to a crawl, and parked on a small, paved public lot at the bottom of the hill, climbing out of the car, he stood on the edge of the lot overlooking the small town on the outskirts of Marseille, the lights of the much larger city in the distance. The setting sun made the Mediterranean Sea appear on fire with red and orange light, but as the sun disappeared beneath the waves, the lights seemed more like star clusters, and the water seemed an inky black void swallowing all warmth.

Moving from the car's hood to the driver's side door, Aahod slipped into the front seat and waited for full dark. He didn't want to risk being seen.

Though most homes in this area were tucked back off the street, behind walls and gates with as many trees and brush surrounding them as there was natural limestone, he needed to remain unnoticed, wanting no one to alert the authorities that a strange Arab man was in the established enclave of foreign expats and residents that had lived in the area for generations.

All these years in America, he had not missed the particular brand of discrimination many White French held towards his North African brothers.

Unlocking his phone Aahod tapped on the digital files Kragen had sent. He reviewed the homes layout as well as the arial view of the property it sat upon. There was no way to approach from the back of the house. There was what looked to be a five-foot stone wall separating the back yard from a sheer drop of jagged stones that could batter, shred flesh, and break bones, as one fell towards the ravine about a hundred and fifty feet below.

Enlarging the pictures of the man, woman, and child, his gaze lingered on the woman. She had warm brown skin and strong, yet delicate, features. Kragen wanted her to know pain, but there was something in her eyes that said she was no stranger to its existence. Aahod knew from Basir's stories that the Kragen's were sadists and murderers but thanks to the man in the picture, only the father remained.

He examined the picture of Zeus, he was of Algerian heritage, but a mutt. He was said to have slaughtered many of Basir's guards that night. Those who had been present and survived had expressed terror, said that the devil walked in the form of a man.

Aahod was not impressed. The guards who died and those who lived were not experts in combat, they were glorified caretakers, defending the property of Prophet Basir, whether that property be material or human.

If he'd been present, been the first to encounter this Zeus, Kragen and all the others would now be alive. There should be no glory given to a man for successfully slaughtering those of limited training.

He would teach Zeus this lesson tonight.

Aahod removed himself from the vehicle when night deepened, when the neighborhood was void of human activity, and only wind and wildlife would be witness to his movements.

Instead of scaling the tall front gate of Zeus's residence, Aahod walked onto the property of the house below it, and hopped the much lower fencing there, entering Zeus's backyard from the neighbor's yard.

Once on the target's land, he didn't move from the place he'd landed, waiting to see if any sensors were triggered.

After nearly ten minutes, with no lights flooding the area and no approaching sirens, Aahod determined that this Zeus didn't believe the residence could be traced back to him. This was his haven. He probably lived here as a regular unassuming man, a friendly seasonal neighbor, not as the killer he was.

Pulling his Nighthawk AAC, he attached his suppressor, and flicked on the TLR-7A light beneath the barrel, scanning the young trees and sparce foliage which cast shadows on the browning grass in some places, gravel and larger stones in others.

Moving slowly towards the house, he stumbled on an almost imperceptible mound of rocks and nearly shouted out in alarm as one of the disturbed stones landed on a patch of earth that sprung an animal trap that would have taken his foot off above the ankle had he kept moving.

His heart pounded in his ears.

He didn't move again until his breathing and heartrate slowed to an acceptable rate.

So, this Zeus was not as lax as he'd assumed.

Aahod took the time to determine his next steps... his literal next steps. He scanned the immediate area for more anomalies, and kneeled to gather two of the larger stones. He tossed one a couple of feet ahead of him, in the direction he wanted to go, stepped there once he'd insured that the area was safe, bending down to retrieve the stone before stepping on the spot where he'd tossed the other.

He was unnerved by the barbaric nature of the trap, but did not rush. It was a slow creep towards the house, but he eventually was less than fifty feet from his destination and hadn't encountered any more dangers.

At twenty feet away he scanned the back of the house. There was a small garden, a grill, a patio area with a wrought iron circular table and two chairs. There was a shed between the patio and back wall. He would not attempt to explore it, given the circumstances.

Dropping the stones that brought him here safely, he stepped onto the paved area surrounding the patio, paused, half-expecting a final trap between here and the houses back door.

"I would not go in there if I were you," a voice warned, behind him.

In one fluid motion Aahod pivoted, aiming his gun in the direction of the voice, searching along the wall at the back of the property with the high-powered light and finding nothing.

Something hit the gun, knocking his hand to the right.

Aahod quickly corrected and fired a couple of stay away shots, but his bullets hit nothing. Nothing living. His heart thumped but he remained alert and steady, reluctant to move toward the ravine for fear of stepping on another of Zeus's traps, but he had to. No threats, no witnesses.

Listening for any auditory indication of the man's location, Aahod continued to scan the area, sweep the ground before stepping towards the back wall.

Once he reached it, knowing it was unlikely someone was on the other side, he took a deep breath, leaned over the edge quickly, and pulled back. He did so again, this time aiming the light into the chasm of darkness, only to have something strike his hand, hard enough to bruise bone, hard enough to weaken his grip before a second hit sent his gun tumbling into the darkness as the light flickered out.

Aahod stumbled back, reaching for his second gun.

"Do not. Please."

He froze, eyes working to adjust to the pitch-black area. He thought he'd be forced into hand-to-hand combat, but no attack came.

As his eyes began delineating objects in the darkness, he focused on something pale further down the wall to his left. A head. The body attached to it was clad black and crouched on top of the stone wall like a gargoyle, but it was very much a man. Platinum hair cropped close to the skull, pale face, framed by black plastic glasses.

The man wasn't Zeus. He had an accent that hailed from some icy Nordic land.

When the man skuttled along the wall like something almost non-human, Aahod thought again to reach for his second gun, but decided that if the man meant him harm, he'd had plenty of opportunity to cause it.

"This is not why you are here, my friend," the voice chastised. But it sounded like the man was speaking to himself.

Aahod felt uncertain. A feeling he hadn't experienced in many years.

"I leave you to your fate now", the man in the dark said. "If you are smart, you will choose life over duty and money. If not, vertu sæl... this means goodbye."

And then he was gone over the other side of the wall. No man would survive that fall, but Aahod wasn't tempted to check.

Walking back to the house, looked inside, determining no one was home, he defied the chill running down his spine and breached the back door, moved through the home cautiously, and smiled once he'd found the most strategic place to lay in wait.

She was tired as shit. Bri was tired as shit; and Sabrina knew this because her niece had become winy and obstinate. Another trait that had to be inherited from her and Sam's mother.

It had been a long afternoon.

After leaving his mother's house, Zeus took them on a

whirlwind tour of Marseille. Parks, cafes, the beach, historical structures. He would've charted a boat and took them out to sea if she hadn't pointed out that it was getting late. It was as if the man believed he'd never get the chance to show them these places again.

Sabrina suspected it was more likely he was trying to tire them out, so they'd want to return home instead of to his mother's for dinner.

If he'd had a slightly less stubborn partner, it probably would've worked.

A wave of nausea hit her, and she took a deep breath and closed her eyes. She wanted to deny the possibility that she was pregnant and until she took the pregnancy test Zeus picked up at the pharmacy, she wouldn't know for sure. But she had a strong constitution, could count on one hand the number of times she'd experienced nausea as an adult.

Maybe her body just didn't like France, even if she did. None of these symptoms existed before France.

The moment her the nausea settled, her stomach growled loud enough to be heard over the activity at the pier. The sun would soon set and Godzuki was hungry. She smiled. She couldn't keep calling her maybe-baby Godzuki.

Leaning her head on Zeus's shoulder, she wrapped her arm around his waist and laughed as Bri, leaning into his other side, tried to push her arm away. They warred for dominance until Bri slid between Zeus and the pier railing and hugged him from the front.

"Let go you, human barnacle!" Sabrina laughed, halfheartedly pushing against Bri.

Zeus looked down at her, his eyes dancing with silver flame, and half-smiled.

Always willing to take the ridiculousness up a notch,

Sabrina stopped trying to get between Bri and Zeus, and instead rounded to his back, hopped up and wrapped her arms around his neck and her legs around his hips and locking her feet together at Brianna's back, sandwiching them all together as Bri shrieked and wiggled, half-heartedly attempting to break free.

"Who's the baddest?!" Sabrina shouted. "Who. Is. The. Baddest?!"

She didn't care that people paused to watch and laugh at them.

Bri stopped resisting and Sabrina, raised a fisted hand in triumph then rested her head against Zeus shoulder and kissed his neck.

"Why is she so *weird*?" Bri lamented.

Zeus squeezed Sabrina's thigh.

"It's her brain," Zeus informed Bri sagely. "It impairs her ability to feel embarrassed when she makes a scene. Remember this, if you're prone to public embarrassment. I try not to give her a reason to misbehave," Zeus said.

"*Me* misbehave? Really!" Sabrina said, hopping back down to the ground.

He nodded. "Really."

'Y'all–"

"Get on your last nerve," Zeus parroted flatty, while Bri finished Sabrina's sentence with scrunched nosed, and frankly, a disrespectful over exaggeration and a "Yeah we heard," as she waved her hand.

"Well, ya do," Sabrina said, nose in the air. "Now let's go have dinner with your family before it gets too late. I want to get home and relax."

Meaning she wanted to get home and take the tests.

Zeus's gaze focused on her breasts. "Relax... I would very much like to go home... and relax."

"I just bet you would," she smiled knowingly, reaching for Briana's hand. "But there's food waiting for us on your mom's table, and we're gonna go eat it."

"I could feed you at home."

"Mind out of the gutter. We're gonna go eat your mother's food, play nice, and after that, if you want to take me home and feed me dessert, I will gladly eat it."

He growled, not seeming to like anything but the dessert part. Her stomach growled back in response.

Zeus lowered his head and raised his brow, then one side of his mouth in a smile.

Wonderful. Father and child were having conversations on a primal level now. This didn't bode well for her.

CHAPTER SIX

They were outside the door for the second time. More people were inside, more voices, but not the sound of raucous gatherings like at Mama's House, the voices were filled with anxiety, anger.

He glared at the door as if it was a thing he could murder.

"Stop growling," Sabrina urged. He didn't.

He slanted a sideways glance at her instead.

"Dinner only," she promised.

"Then we get the fuck out of here."

"You can't say bad words in front of kids," Bri said with wide eyes. He scowled at her too. "Just remember, you love me, and you can't kill the people you love."

"Is that a rule?" he asked Sabrina.

"It is absolutely a rule."

"I refused to love anyone other than you. And you," he said to Bri before banging on the door. "And any of my—"

"Kaiju? Hell spawn?" Sabrina innocently.

She was not innocent.

"Wild Things?" Bri offered.

He clenched his molars together and lowered his head.

They were not cute. Or amusing.

He cracked his neck from side to side. Inhaled and exhaled slowly.

Ok, they were cute. But he didn't need to say it, they already knew they were.

"We eat, we leave," Sabrina said soberly, as someone approached the door from the other side. Maybe she was finally willing to let go of this fantasy of a happy-ever-after with these people.

The door opened before, and the woman stood there.

Her smile seemed forced.

He forced a smile back and she flinched.

His smile disappeared.

"It's good to see you again, Zahira," Sabrina said. "Sorry we're so late, I think Zeus took us to every arrondissement in Marseille."

"Did you take them to St. Catherine's?" the woman asked tentatively.

Did you revisit the place I abandoned you? Was that what she was really asking?

He stared at her.

His fingers began to twitch rhythmically as if the fire igniting inside his chest was reanimating digits that had been frozen in rigor.

"Why would I?" he asked, tilting his head, curious for her response.

"I... you...." Zahira stammered.

"Let them in Zahra," the old woman said behind her. "What, are we so uncivilized that we speak of family business in public?"

"Oui, Mamon. I have been rude, please come in," she said, coaxing them forward. "Please, please."

Zeus was the last to enter.

He didn't like the woman's eyes. They felt desperate, like she desperately wanted something from him that he wasn't willing to give.

Inside the house, he saw the two children they'd seen in the courtyard, as well as the man who'd eyed Sabrina at the elevator earlier.

"This is your step-brother David, and his children Ada and Michelle."

Zeus gazed at the man unwaveringly. Family or not, he'd carve this motherfucker into bite sized pieces if he looked at Sabrina with anything other than familial respect.

Zeus gaze slanted towards the two girls.

"Where's their mother?"

David reddened and cleared his throat. "On the way, yes. She had work. She's an..." he looked to Zahira. "How do you say...infirmiere?"

"Nurse," his mother clarified.

"I'm fluent in French," Zeus informed her. "Raised here the first few years of my life."

Zahira's eyes widened in surprised then fell away. The fissures of anxiety and guilt were threatening to fracture her mask of hyper-happiness into pieces. But he was willing to play it her way for now. Her house, her rules.

"You've met my mother and my husband, but this is my husband's brother, Jean, and his wife Lanis."

Zeus nodded.

"Nice to meet you all," Sabina smiled, because she had the patience and skill for this bullshit.

Instead of adapting his more guarded stance, Bri followed Sabrina's example and walked over to the two girls.

"Tu parle Anglaise?" she asked in decent enough French. She'd been practicing the phrase all day. Nearly every business owner, stranger, and tour guide they encountered.

The girls looked to their father before responding, then nodded at Bri.

"Hi," she smiled. "I'm Briana, but people call me Bri. My mom Sabrina is the original Bri, and my dad's name is Zeus. Like the God."

Zeus glanced at Sabrina, her shrug was almost imperceptibly. They'd never had a conversation with Briana about the role she wanted them to assume in her life. She'd apparently made the decision on her own.

He was officially a father. Huh.

Being claimed by her this way locked something into place he'd thought was already a given. They'd claimed each other that first day on the Jace's porch, he'd given her her soul blade. But to hear that she wanted him not just as her uncle, her guardian, but as her parent, her father.... She was his for the rest of his life. In a way, he didn't fully comprehend what it would mean, but he was her father, this life and after. He couldn't imagine giving up that gift for anything.

He turned flat eyes towards the woman done just that when he was voiceless. Defenseless.

Violent energy burned through him.

He moved his fingers against his thigh, this dance was one created after he'd met Sabrina. One that re-established the pleasures of life when all he wanted to do was invoke death.

The adults in the room grew pensive. The children talked with animation, but Briana's gaze slid towards him, aware and watchful. Her ability to be vigilant without appearing to, was impressive.

"Dinner smells wonderful," Sabrina said enthusiastically.

The smile his mother gave her was genuine, relieved.

"We eat very soon".

"Is there someplace we can wash up?"

"Oui, yes, come." Nabeela said.

She guided them across the living-room in the opposite direction of the kitchen, passed the dining area, to the wide hall beyond.

"The children, I will take to the kitchen to wash, this is, okay?" Zahira called out.

Apparently, it was because Sabrina nodded and pulled him along as she followed Nabeela. Zeus turned to watch Bri walk towards the kitchen with Zahira and the other girls. When Nabeela opened the door to the bathroom, Sabrina walked in and he entered behind her, firmly shutting the door.

Sabrina used the toilet, complaining that *'this water is running through me'*. She was trying to drink more of it *'just in case I'm pregnant'*. She was. Zeus washed his hands, only half listening, and was back in the hallway, watching for Briana to come back into his line of sight.

Sabrina exited the bathroom, and he didn't wait for either woman as he walked through the flat, back towards the living room. Sabrina called his name and he stopped, the other adults in the room looked at him warily.

He looked at them one by one, cool with the idea of them never saying a word.

Fuck these people, he thought, as Sabrina drew closer.

There was another knock at the door and David rushed to open it as Zahira exited the kitchen laughing and teasing Bri and the other girls as she helped them dry their hands.

When Zahira's gaze went to the door her eyes widened and she froze.

Zeus had a blade in each hand, flicked his wrist in a horizontal slice motion, signaling for Sabrina to stop advancing.

Swinging his gaze to the man standing in the open doorway, Zeus squinted, tilted his head. He tightened his fists around his blades, then re-sheathed them; only the man and Sabrina had witnessed his blades' brief appearance. Everyone else was focused on the man who crossed over the threshold without invitation and stepped fully into the room.

"Why... how did you...?" Zahira whispered in French, never completing her sentence.

The man didn't acknowledge her, his electric silver white blue eyes, resembling an Alaskan Husky's, hit Zeus like an electric current.

"I've come to see my son," the man said, his voice as rough as his appearance. The man's skin was a degree or two darker than Zeus's. His maybe once all dark blond hair was filled with mostly glinting gray strands that were held in a bunch at the top of his head by a loose top knot. His hair would've fallen just below his shoulders if free.

The man was broader than Zeus, his muscles denser, with worn tattoos covering the swarthy skin along his arms and chest. He wore black cargo pants and black boots, and most curious of all, a stained dove gray sleeveless t-shirt with traces of... blood.

If the man never said a word, Zeus would've known who he was. Felt the sameness, the instinctual cellular recognition that never materialized with Zahira.

"Nuns and priests said my father wasn't a man," Zeus reflected to himself. "Mostly said he was the devil."

A corner of his father's mouth tilted up. Zeus heard Sabrina's sharp inhalation as she stepped alongside Zeus. "As if mere men can distinguish Gods and Devils," he said, his French didn't have the same socio-economic status as the others in the room.

A full smile spread across his father's face. "I am more than Gods and Devils," he said, switching to thickly accented English. "I am Sirius Sideris, the brightest celestial being in the night sky, *your* father, and you are my son."

"I can definitely see, *and hear,* the family resemblance." Sabrina said.

Zeus lowered his head and inhaled as the man moved towards them.

His father *definitely* smelled of blood and death.

The fine hairs covering Zeus's skin rose. He narrowed his gaze but allowed the big Greek to approach, wrap his arms around Zeus in a fierce hug. Zeus gazed over at Sabrina to clock her reaction, hoping this was the reunion she imagined. He relaxed in his father embrace and returned the embrace. Sabrina teared up and Zeus realized it wasn't his parents' or his family's reactions that she was anticipating.

It was his.

Zeus wondered if they would be able to get on with their future now that she believed he was loved and wanted and accepted, that he knew he was a child who had a place in his parents' hearts.

With a quick dance of his fingers, he reached beneath his father's shirt, feeling pride when he pulled free the hidden object and held it up.

"He's got a blade," he showed Sabrina.

He was impressed.

"Much loved and often used blade," Sirius stated roughly. "Tool of trade."

Stepping back, Sirius reclaimed possession of his cleaver and held it up. There was a familiar gleam in his father's eyes as he stroked the steal. "I am butcher. Best in all of France."

"I've also been called a butcher. One of the best in the world," Zeus said.

Only difference was he didn't carve up dead things.

"I am Sirius," his father smiled. "Which makes me best and brightest butcher in universe."

"This must be where you get your humility from," Sabrina said.

"Who needs humility when there is truth," Sirius scoffed.

Sabrina laughed. Zeus turned his gaze back to the older man with the freaky eyes. "You I could add to my list of...." He stopped himself. Too soon to add to the list of people he couldn't kill or hurt. "...my list of people I like."

Sirius gripped both sides of Zeus's face and kissed each cheek.

"Yeah," he said taking a step back, about to let Sirius know he didn't actually like to be touched when Briana shyly squeezed between them and looked up at Sirius as if he *was* a star. "Hi."

"My kid, Briana." Zeus motioned to Bri. "My woman, Sabrina."

Sirius picked up Bri and held her and Sabrina in a tight squeeze, then gazed down at them as if they were the earth and the moon. Zeus sighed, they kinda were.

"My son. My family," Sirius said, the moisture in his eyes made them glisten like ice.

"Come, come, let us eat," Zahira interrupted anxiously.

"I could eat a cow," Sabrina said patting her stomach. She was really patting his child.

He reached out and patted him too. "They'll eat," Zeus told Zahira. "I'm not hungry."

He'd eat when he got home; didn't like to eat a lot of food he or the Brood didn't make, and he'd already filled his quota of other people's food today.

"Sorry for interrupting, Zahira," Sirius said. "It is good to know you are doing well." He nodded at Zahira's mother. "Thank you calling. I will go—"

"No," Zeus said, resisting the urge to grab the man by the shoulder to keep him there. He didn't know why it was important, but he needed him to stay.

"There is plenty of food, you must join us Sirius, it is the least we could do," the old woman said.

"Thank you, but I am also not hungry. But I stay, merci, sit with my son."

Zahira directed them to a pristine white satin settee with large ethereal flowers, their stems painted gold. The settee arms were plumply cushioned but the wood that made up the legs were carved delicately and spindled.

Father and son eyed each other before lowering themselves onto the cushions. They looked as comfortable as two horses sitting on a spun glass stool.

Zeus leaned forward, resting his forearms on his widespread thighs, lacing his fingers together, as he looked out of the window across the room with the balcony overlooking the city. Maintaining his balance, in the event the seating caved, he watched as Sabrina and Briana were placed beside each other on the far side of the table. This allowed him to watch their every expression.

"Do you speak Greek?" Sirius asked.

"No."

"Is no problem, I will teach you."

Sabrina and Bri ate and talked to the family like they had known them for years. They were both good at pretending. He knew they weren't as relaxed as they appeared because they continued to visually check on him and Sirius.

"Your woman, she is beautiful," Sirius said.

Zeus grunted his agreement.

"Do you love her... as much as she loves you?"

"Nah, way more," Zeus said

"This is good, this is how it should be. Me, I cared for your mother very much once. But it was the love of children, too fragile to fight off poison."

"Relationship wasn't blessed by the spirits," Zeus concluded.

Sirius leaned forward and looked from Zahira to her mother.

"No, no blessings... curses perhaps."

Zeus side-eyed him, wondering if his conception was the curse.

Those were the last words shared as they watched the exchange of the others at the dinner table, followed by the clean-up.

Sabrina relaxed and seemed to connect with everyone, even with David once his wife showed up. Briana on the other hand seemed to use him as a touchstone, coming over periodically, leaning against him, bringing the other two children to him.

There was an argument between the children about who had the best father. Bri obviously did.

Zahira called the children to the kitchen with the promise of sweets and they raced away. Very loudly. In the kitchen the kids quieted, and Zahira walked out. Seconds later, there were screams and the other two children ran out.

Zeus sat up when Bri didn't emerge with them, but resisted the urge to approach the children when he heard them accuse Bri of trying to cut them with a knife.

Moments later Bri exited the kitchen, walking over to Zeus with her head hanging down.

"I'm sorry," she whispered. "I just wanted to show them my gift."

Your own blade, one that chose you, was something to be proud of.

He cut his eyes towards Sabrina. If he said the wrong thing there'd be an issue.

"Blade Spirits aren't here to impress those who can't even comprehend their existence," he said to Bri. "Only share your blades when they want to be seen... or felt? Was it either?"

"No," she glared across the room at the other children then whispered in his ear. "I didn't try to cut them, they just got scared. If I wanted to cut them, I would have."

He knew her skill well enough to know that she was telling the truth.

Sabrina stood beside the dining-room table looking at them both with her arms crossed.

He narrowed his gaze when she didn't approach or intervene.

This was a test. She wanted to see if he could parent appropriately.

Zeus lowered his head.

"Apologize," he muttered, low enough for only Bri and possibly Sirius, to hear. "Then cry. Quickest way out. Then we go home and watch movies."

Bri walked away, her head still hanging low, stopped in front of the two girls, never looking up.

"I'm sorry I scared you," she said softly.

Then she covered her face with her hands and her shoulders began to shake. And her tears... her tears sounded real, real enough to make Zeus stand, his fingers moving at an accelerated rate, his blades calling out to be seen. And felt.

Sabrina picked Bri up, and the child wrapped her arms tight around Sabrina's neck, her legs wrapping around her hips as she cried in the nook of Sabrina's shoulder.

"She's had a long day and a lot of excitement. We're going to go–"

Zahira and her family protested but it was the exact outcome he wanted. If he had to....

His watch vibrated.

He went still, blocking out all unnecessary stimuli to focus what that vibration communicated. There was a threat at his home. *We must eliminate threats. Protect.*

He steered Sabrina away from the noise of this family, gathered her and Bri's belongings and moved them to the front door. He opened it, made sure there was no one waiting in the hallway, and guided them through it, ignoring the protests, the apologies. He heard Sabrina rush out a "thank you" and "goodbye" before he shut the door and pulled them down the hall behind him.

The door to the flat opened and he heard his mother ask in French, "Sirius, you are leaving? We never had a chance to talk."

Zeus pushed the button for the elevator and looked back to see his father step into the hall.

"I go with my son," was all Sirius said, and closed the door.

No words were exchanged between any of them until they were on the sidewalk. Sirius followed them to the SUV and Zeus frowned at him over the roof of the car as Sabrina and Bri climbed inside.

"I will watch over our girls. You go to eliminate danger, yes?"

Yes.

Zeus's first instinct was to hunt. When a threat needed to be eliminated, he considered the ways it could be done, anticipated the dance, the aftermath of carnage.

But his father's words reminded him that when they reached home and he left the car, Sabrina and Bri would be vulnerable. Back in California, he trusted the Brood to keep Sabrina safe when he wasn't with her. Was he ready to extend that same trust to a man he knew almost nothing about?

His silver gaze tangled with Sirius's white-blue dog star eyes.

Instinct said yes. Blade Spirits said *it is decided*.

Sirius knew Zeus was responding to danger and he was here, willing to face it with them without question.

And he's a butcher, Zeus thought, knew how to carve up flesh. And the cleaver he carried at his back pulsated with power.

Zeus nodded and got into the driver's seat. The back door opened and closed, and Sirius buckled up beside Briana.

"You are very good at pretending," Sirius said to Bri as they pulled away.

"I was in *three* school plays last year. I was the best Annie my teacher had even seen. Pretending is easy for me."

"Problem with pretending is that sometimes you can forget who you are, and that only hurts you in the long run." Sabrina said gently.

There was a lesson imbedded in her words, but Zeus wasn't in a space to figure it out. Plus, the lesson wasn't for him, it was for Briana.

"Be ready," he warned Sabrina.

She needed to focus on what was coming, not on whatever she was trying to teach Bri.

"I'm ready," she said, shaking her head. "But these sons of.... why won't they just leave us the hell alone?"

"Vengeance. Powerlessness. Rage," Zeus offered.

"Maxim got better than what he deserved."

Zeus had beheaded the son.

If someone hurt his child, the world would bleed until that someone was eliminated from it. He understood Kragen the father's motivation; more now than ever. But, as a father himself now, it was his job to make sure that Kragen and his Consortium didn't get what they wanted.

Only what they deserved.

"I'll park at the bottom of the hill," he told Sabrina, when they entered his neighborhood. Looking in the rear-view mirror, he saw that Briana was asleep, but his father's electric gaze was locked onto him. It was good he was here. Sirius wasn't afraid of blood. The spirits said trust him. He would. But he trusted Sabrina more. He leaned towards her, she met him halfway. When her lips touched his he felt an added level of power.

"I'll hunt alone," he said, turning onto the road that led to his house. He pulled into the small lot at the bottom of the hill that usually only residents used, and parked yards from a black sedan. "Stay ready."

"Stay safe," Sabrina said, pulling two bowies from beneath her seat.

Stepping out into the cool night, he walked over to the other car, checked the plates, gazed inside. This wasn't a resident's car. He rounded to the back of the SUV and stripped out of his shirt, socks, and shoes.

The back passenger door opened, and Sirius joined him.

"My life for theirs," Sirius promised.

"Yeah, let's hope it doesn't come to that. I got questions."

"Good. Return, my son, and you will have your answers." He pulled his butcher's knife. "Good hunting, may the fates protect you."

Aahod wrapped the night around him, waiting in the recesses of the downstairs hall across from the kitchen. Whether the killer and his family came through the front door or back, he would see them almost immediately from here.

After checking the house, he'd reengaged the lock to the back door, searched both levels to confirm he was alone, and made sure the upstairs windows were unbreachable by any means other than breaking the panes. The killer didn't know he was here, but killers like him, being what they were, prepared for danger. If the window was broken, Aahod would hear it and know which direction to move to complete his assignment.

He wasn't the kind of assassin that longed for a *worthy battle*, he preferred precision, efficiency. To slide in and out with no sign of disruption other than the bullet hole ending his target's life.

Yes, the man he would kill, and the child he would drug and bind and secure in the trunk of his car and take to Kragen's yacht. The woman... she was not a good woman, and he would kill her but unlike Kragen's fantasy, he would not violate her. He detested the perversions against women that Kragen, and those like him, participated in. It was not his way.

Aahod didn't know what caused his senses to go on alert,

but he focused his attention to the sounds of the house, the sounds of the night, felt a cool stream of air, faint, that hadn't caressed him until that moment.

The wind had picked up outside, so the draft could be due to poor insulation, but he didn't stay alive by assuming the best. He'd closed the doors upstairs and they hadn't been opened, there were no footfalls from above at all, and the steps that connected upstairs with downstairs were creaky in places, no sound of movement there.

Aahod contemplated walking backwards to the well-stocked pantry and hiding inside where there was no option for his target to escape. But that would only prolong his time here. He leaned forward, gun tight against his leg, barrel pointed towards the ground.

Nothing moved within his direct line of vision.

But he knew with certainty that he was no longer alone.

Perhaps the night phantom had returned. If so, he'd feel the consequences of his continued interference.

No matter. Aahod remained rooted in place. Tonight, he would be the spider, patiently waiting for whatever unfortunate insect got entangled inside his web of death.

The front door creaked open and Aahod pulled back against the wall, just enough to see what was coming, but not enough to be seen.

He waited for someone to come through, but the door never opened farther than a foot. He continued to wait, ever patient, only to be startled by the almost imperceptible swoosh of the back door opening.

He was sure no one slipped through but from this vantage point he could only make out a small section of the door; most of the space within that back room wasn't visible.

Someone was toying with him, attempting to lure him

from his hiding spot, but he was not so easily played, his skills honed by years of practice.

Smiling slightly, he looked ahead, towards the kitchens back wall. If anything moved either left or right, the first thing the intruder felt would be the impact of his bullet. The next, nothing.

A bead of sweat slipped down Aahod's spine. He held position, waiting, but nothing more happened.

He would not move, would not expose himself. But he felt uncertainty. Was this the killer or was it the platinum haired phantom, or was it someone else entirely, someone else hired for the job? There was no indication of the woman or child, no opening gate, no sound of a car driving into the yard.

More and more he believed it was the phantom, but this time the strange man would not have the upper hand. Aahod was not exposed as he'd been in the yard, he knew where–

The air seemed to sigh in disappointment.

Too late.

Still, he spun, aimed... but it was too late. The large shadowy figure hadn't moved, but Aahod felt a tingling sensation at his elbow, frowned when he looked down and realized his arm was no longer attached, was laying on the ground, with his hand still clutching the gun.

Aahod growled, pulled his bowie, and lunged, focused on striking out, focused on disabling his opponent, focused on killing him.

All offensive attacks resulted in him being slashed over and over again, from every direction. It was as if he fought a being of sharpened steal. Something blunt hit him against the side of his face and he momentarily lost the vision in one eye. The side of his head felt numb. Moving backwards towards the kitchen, he was now focused on surviving, focused on breathing, focused on not bleeding to death.

Squinting at the shadowed man, he tryed to find him in the bowels of the hall, but blood further blurred what darkness obscured from his vision. Aahod's breathing felt labored, his chest was burning. Had his lung been punctured? He didn't even recall being stabbed in the chest.

"Hidden traps," he breathed out. "I thought I avoided them all, but here... this place," he struggled to remain upright against the kitchen island. "This place *is* the trap. And I'd entered so confidently." He looked towards the heavens, his laugh incredulous. "I shut the door to my own cage."

He tried to pull himself upright, but his body wouldn't support its weight.

"I will die here," he realized.

"You don't have to."

Aahod's gaze snapped back towards the dark hall. He tried to clear the blood from his eyes, wanting to see, needing to see the face of his killer.

As if granted a dying wish, the figure was released from the protection of shadows. Aahod regretted that he hadn't asked for a different wish. What stood before him would have struck terror into the heart of lesser men. He'd initially thought demon; the man looked like he'd been skinned alive. Then Aahod realized that it was not exposed flesh he was seeing, but skin, skin so saturated with blood, his blood, that it appeared that way.

The killer reached towards the wall and soft lights flooded the hallway, exposing the hellish scene the darkness protected him from.

His arm lay on the ground. Blood was everywhere, he had cause to believe that it was only his blood. His assassination sites were never this grisly, they were pristine, if not for the bodies.

"You don't have to die. Because I have a family, I'm evolving," the killer, Zeus, said.

The blood dripping from the two large blades said otherwise.

"Tell me where Kragen is, and I'll return you to him alive. If not," the blades returned to the ready. "We finish the dance. I'll send you to him in pieces and like with your arm you will be alive when I do it."

"I have no loyalty to Basir's colleague, brother."

The killer scowled down at the ground. He was very strange.

"Who is your father?" the killer asked.

"Samir."

"And your mother?

"Maritesh."

"Then we're not brothers. Choose."

"Bag my arm please, and tend my wounds if you want me alive before we reach Kragen."

"Don't really give a shit, just want to reach Kragen," the killer said, gripping both blades in one hand as he used the other to pull a mobile from his back pocket and make a call. "Come home. Take Bri upstairs, no one comes to the kitchen. Because... blood. No, he's alive. You too."

The killer was efficient and methodical; getting him out of the house through the back door just as the front gate opened. From the entire journey to Aahod's car to Kragen's yacht, he wondered if Zeus would keep his word, allow him to live, but if he died tonight it had to be the will of Allah, so there would be no attempts at fleeing or attacking... unless an opportunity arose that couldn't be ignored.

The berth the GPS directed them to was in a more remote area. When Zeus parked and left the car, Aahod knew there would be no better time to escape, and although he was no longer interested in money or duty, he was weakened from blood loss. He must have lost consciousness because when he came to, he was laid out on a bed that was obviously below deck, the sounds of undulating waters was soothing, reminded him of his childhood on the beach, laughing with his brother and–

"Kragen is not here."

Ah, the killer was still with him. Looking to the side he saw Zeus watching him with his back to the corner.

"He will be," Aahod assured.

"For your sake, hope that's true."

Then he left.

Not just gone from the room but, Aahod sensed, gone from the yacht, leaving Aahod to live or die at Kragen's whim. He did not have faith in Kragen's whim, just needed to rest for a moment, then call Basir. All would be well.

Closing his eyes, he took a deep breath and harnessed what little energy remained before he would attempt to stand. He envisioned retrieving his arm left in the ice bucket, but even it was not necessary to live. He would return to his home land and live out the rest of his days at his small family home close to the beach.

Preparing for pain, he opened his eyes and struggled to sit upright. He froze at the sight beside him. Crouched on the floor next to the bed was the bespeckled platinum haired phantom he'd shot at in Zeus yard.

"You were not smart, my friend." The man shook his head woefully. "Duty, money; do they now feel worth your life?"

No, Aahod thought, no they did not.

As the man unfolded, rising above him, Aahod wondered if he'd ever been the spider. Then he wondered if he'd ever seen a spider die in its own web.

"Vertu sæl," the phantom said, donning gloves that resemble black claws of leather and steal.

Aahod remembered the other man's words meant goodbye.

Goodbye.

He had no time to verbalize his own farewell. His throat was the first body part ripped from him, and when the claws plunged into his chest, he was grateful for the darkness, grateful that it spared him from what else was to become of the physical form he'd once possessed.

CHAPTER SEVEN

I t took a while to get Bri settled after Sabrina got her bathed and in bed.

"But we were supposed to do movie night... with popcorn," Bri reminded her on the brink of tears. These tears weren't fake and had little to do with movie night.

"We'll still have it, just another night."

"What if he needs us and we're not there to help him? What if he gets hurt... or dies?"

Sabrina swallowed, understanding Bri's fear and grief. She sat on the bed, resting her back against the headboard and stretching her legs out along its length. Bri's head rested on the pillow near Sabrina's hip.

Reaching over, Sabrina stroked the downy soft hair at Bri's temple with her thumb.

In the little time since Bri had learned of Sabrina's existence, had learned of the Brood, she'd been taught to be more aware, more alert, but Bri was already smart and acutely attuned to those around her. Awareness strengthened Bri's safety, and yes, Sabrina wanted her to learn to take care of herself, but she also wanted her to remain a free-spirited child, wanted her to feel safe without worrying about losing someone else.

"He'll come home," Sabrina assured her. She smiled and tried to lighten the mood. "Hasn't he said over and over that he's a God?"

"But he's not though, not for real."

"You're right, he's not; he's capable of getting hurt."

Sabrina remembered the levels of abuse he'd endured when he'd been captured, remembered her fear and desperation over the possibility of losing him. "But Zeus *is* special. So special he was able to make love grow in a place inside me I thought was dead. He'll come back, and we'll have our movie day, just chilling at home together as a family. We don't even have to change out of our pjs if we don't want to. Okay?"

"Can we have kettle-corn popcorn?"

"Only if you sleep!" she said tickling her. *Probably not the best wind down routine*, she thought stretching out beside Bri, their heads sharing the same pillow.

"I'll have Zeus come up and say goodnight when he comes home."

"Even if I'm sleep?"

"Even if."

"Is Sirius going to stay the night?" Bri was fighting sleep, but that didn't stop her from thinking about the older man who was already downstairs cleaning.

"I have a feeling that he won't be leaving for a while."

"That's good," Bri said, closing her eyes.

Quiet stretched between them so long Sabrina rose to leave the bedroom.

"When I showed my gift earlier," Bri said, opening her eyes. "I just wanted them to see how pretty she is."

"Well," Sabina sat up, her tone stern, face serious. "I'm sorry too."

Bri looked fearful.

Wrong façade, Sabrina thought, not intending to trigger the child, but she continued because mothers had to set limits with their children to protect them didn't they? "Our family is not like other families, Briana. What's normal for us won't be normal for a lot of people. So, when you're think of doing something you're not sure about, think about how Mrs. Jace would react and let that reaction guide you. For example, if Mrs. Jace was at Zahira's house, would you have shown your gift?"

"Oh *nooooo,*" Bri said with wide eyes. "Mrs. Jace don't play that."

Sabrina laughed, tucking Bri in the covers. "Exactly."

Bri quieted and looked away, her fingers began to worry the edge of the cover.

"Are you and Zeus mad at me for saying you're my parents?"

"Sam will always be your mother, and I'm..." she remembered her sister's quiet smile before Kragen III took it. "I hate that you two never got to meet in person, to know just how wonderful you both are."

"Me too. All I ever really wanted was for her to come see me. Is it bad to want regular parents, like other kids."

"Well, you got parents, but regular, that's a stretch."

"Irregular parents?"

"Totally irregular," Sabrina said, leaning over to kiss Bri on the forehead. "Now go to sleep so you'll be prepared to do battle over which movies we watch tomorrow."

"I'll win," Bri said.

"Doubt it," Sabina sang out as she made her way to the door. "Night my beautiful, strong, smart, spirited girl; see you in the morning."

"Goodnight, Ma."

Sabina nearly smashed her finger as she closed Briana's door. *Ma?* She was used to life coming at her fast, but this shit.... And it would only get more surreal if the pregnancy test results came back positive. But she'd wait for Zeus before she went down that particular rabbit hole.

Back in the kitchen, she was surprised to see that Sirius had already cleaned most of it.

"You are *fast*," she said, staring at the mini-miracle Sirius had pulled off.

"I am butcher, many ways to remove blood. This? This is easy, simple, thing."

"Days after meeting your son, I was cleaning blood off just about every surface of my kitchen," she told him, peering at the products he was using. "He has an issue with people invading his space."

"He is good protector, is my son?"

"Relentlessly so," she said.

Sirius nodded once. "Is in his blood," he said, pouring a white powdery substance on a spot glistening with blood.

"Meat tenderizer?" she frowned.

"Good for blood stains, as well... how do you say... oxygen peroxide, oui, et oxidized bleach. Never use with hot water, this is no good."

"Should've known Zeus's father would know how to remove blood."

Sirius straightened, and she chastised herself, wondering if she'd offended him.

"Je suis un père. This is..." He shook his head in wonder. "Amazing thing."

She smiled, exhaling, as she grabbed a rag.

The night she'd suggested Zeus find his birth mother, it was her attempt to connect him with someone else who could love him, who could care for him if anything happened to her. The Brood, they would be there in their own way, but she knew their way wasn't necessarily healthy. She loved them, but it wasn't.

A mother who left her infant son with a ring to remind him of her though... Sabrina knew she would love him if she met him, and beneath Zahira's pain, Sabrina saw love inside it. She didn't know if Zeus was willing to work his way to it, but unlike that night all those weeks ago, he now had Bri and Sirius. And unlike what *might* be with Zahira, Zeus was already bound to his father, otherwise he never would have trusted the older man to stay. In less than an hour he'd trusted Sirius with her and Bri's life.

He hadn't even trusted her that quickly.

As she and Sirius worked to restore the kitchen and back room, so that there was no visible signs of violence for Bri to wake up to, he wanted to know how she and Zeus met and why they'd come to France. She was honest. She told him everything from their first encounter in the warehouse, all the way to why they were currently cleaning blood out of the house. She'd even started to tell him bits of her own life.

When Zeus came through the front door, it took everything Sabrina had not to run and examine every inch of his body, to make sure he wasn't critically injured. Instead, she moved from the backroom, approached him sedately as he entered the kitchen, and methodically inspected every inch of his upper body for wounds. There was only one on his upper arm haphazardly bound in gauze.

"Let me look at that and clean it properly."

As a one-time EMT, they both knew she was more than qualified.

"Briana?" Zeus asked.

"More upset that you went off without us than she was about not having movie night, but we worked it out."

He frowned at her as she unwrapped the old bandaging.

"What did you tell her?"

"That you were probably crying in a corner somewhere waiting for us to rescue you."

He snorted, his eye color shifted from tempered steal to liquid silver. It was the only warning she got before he kissed her. Deeply, unescapably. She wound her arms around his hips and pulled him tighter. It was only the sound of Sirius behind her that made her pull away and rest her head against Zeus's chest. The rhythm of his heart was steady and strong.

"Was it Kragen?" She asked.

"Nah, his assassin. No, Basir's assassin, but Kragen contracted him. His name is Aahod. He took me to the yacht where he was supposed to bring Bri, but no one was there. Didn't wait around, but I let Aahod live, his reward for coop-erating. That's what you call evolving, right?"

She laughed against the peaks and valleys of his warm chest.

"You love me so much," he said, kissing the top of her head.

She looked up at him and he kissed her again.

"I love your *blades*, but you," she shrugged. "Hell, I guess."

Neither had to guess. They both knew.

"Kragen wasn't on the boat, but I got his scent. Tomorrow

is family movie day, but tomorrow night I'm reuniting the father with the son."

"As it should be," she said, wanting the threat of the Kragen's gone.

"You're devolving, huh?"

"Nooo, I'm simply wishing him an end to his misery; if he's missing his son so much, I agree that they should be together in hell."

"In other words, yes."

"In other words, hell yes."

"I'm making a place in the back room for your father to sleep; he didn't want to take the bedroom upstairs, says he needs to be close to the ground."

"My father. He's more than a butcher. I can tell."

She laughed. "Oh my God, you really don't want to admit that you're just a man!"

"Keep up the disrespect," he said, walking towards the bathroom. "And you won't be riding the lightning tonight."

"Oh, you think you're threatening me? Please, I know you, which means I know just how much your little lightning rod needs to find its home in the thundercloud that is my body."

He muttered something under his breath, and she grinned. She might not know what he said, but she knew it was something disparaging her woman's brain. But he knew she was right, which is why he glared before entering the bathroom.

Maybe it would be a good night to remind him about the benefits of being a flesh and blood man.

Zeus kneeled beside Bri's bed and watched her.

He never could've slept this deeply as a kid. Would've

sensed the moment he wasn't alone in his space, remembered never wanting to wake up to unexpected surprises.

But that had been his life. He didn't want it to be hers. She'd experienced more loss and heart break than he ever had at her age, so he'd give her movie nights with Sabrina, give it to himself too.

He tapped her nose.

Her eyes fluttered behind her lids before opening. She smiled, captured his finger, and held it.

"I don't cry in corners waiting to be rescued," he told her. "Just so we're clear."

"I can't even imagine it," she said, joy and relief danced in her eyes.

He got it then, Sabrina had been teasing him.

"Sabrina thinks she's funny."

"She's kinda funny."

He arched his brow.

"She *is*." She shrugged her small shoulders as if that truth couldn't be denied. "But you're funny too."

"I am."

Her brow arched and her expression flattened.

He'd worn that expression many times.

"No, you're not, I was just being polite."

"Go back to sleep."

She giggled into her pillow.

He didn't have to be the funniest person in the family. Though he obviously was.

He leaned over and placed a kiss on her temple, where the fine hairs were softer than anything he'd ever felt. She wound her arms around his neck and held him tight.

"I love you," she whispered, pressing her face into his

neck. "I know you're like super deadly, but I want you to be safe forever."

"Death comes for everybody."

"Oh my God, you're so bad at this!" she cried out, pulling away.

The side of his mouth ticked up. The kid really was dramatic.

"Just like with a blade, you gotta practice to get better. I'll be around, kid. Who else'll train you and Godzuki to cut through all challenges, when I'm to old to do it."

That time would never come, but he believed it's what she needed to hear.

He was proved a right when she settled back down and gazed up at him from her pillow.

"Can I call Sirius grandpaw, or Pop Pop, or *grandpere*?" she ended in perfectly accented French.

He didn't even know what *he* should call him.

"Get back to you on that," he said, rising and half closing the door as he left the room.

When he went downstairs, their bedroom door was closed. He stood there listening to Sabrina moving around on the other side but didn't go in. For some reason she'd been shocked when both tests came back positive... as if he hadn't told her multiple times throughout the day that they would. She didn't appreciate his feedback.

Giving her a few more minutes to let her brain come to terms with reality, he walked to the backroom where Sirius sat on the pull out with his knees up around his chest. His large frame dwarfed the queen-sized mattress.

"May not want to stay," Zeus said. "There'll be more blood."

Sirius looked at him, his electric white-blue eyes as compelling as the brightest star in the night sky. Zeus often gazed up at the dog-star when he slept in nature on a clear night.

"Ta mére, did she tell you about us? À propos de moi?"

Zeus shook his head. "She cried a lot."

Sirius smiled slightly. "The woman she is now, I don't know, mais, when young, she was timid little hummingbird."

"And you?" Zeus asked, sitting on the floor back to the wall.

"Me?" Sirius looked down at his large hands. "Je n'ai pas suffi... I wasn't enough." he translated, maybe wanting to be sure Zeus understood him. "Greek, rough, stinking of blood and fish. The son of a butcher, oui, grandson of a fisherman."

Zeus pulled his black blade, let it move between his fingers as he listened.

Zahira's father had been French military when she was conceived. He'd married Nabeela before Zahira was born.

"In this time, now, maybe no problem? But Algerian woman and French officer during the War of Liberation, un petit problem, eh?"

His father's gaze grew distant. "I think he wasn't good man. Wanted—" he fisted both hands to demonstrate.

"To control," Zeus guessed.

"Ouai, control. Possess like he owned their life, especially the mother."

Zeus was reminded of Sabrina's relationship with her dead ex.

"Zahira, he try to erase." He made a slicing motion. "Cut her mother's blood and heritage from her and make her the perfect provincial princess. She was very afraid of life when we met, unsure of who she was, taught to be perfect French girl yet he treated her as less. When we meet, I was her first freedom." He smiled evilly. "Her father hated me because I was rough boy. But I made her smile. She was always so nervous, waiting to be attacked, not bodily, but with words you see. I help her begin to believe in her. I think her father hated me for this most of all."

Sirius smiled and Zeus could imagine his appeal as a younger man. Devilment, seduction, violence, they were all there as he spoke of the past.

"Her father tried to stop us, tried to keep us apart, but kids find a way, eh?"

Zeus would keep Bri too busy with training to *find a way*. He'd teach her to kill boys instead of kissing them.

His blade stilled as a new thought entered his mind.

"You made her smile, then you left her when she was pregnant."

Sirius abandoned his awkward perch on the bed and slid down to the floor stretching his legs out beside Zeus's.

"Mon père, he was big man. Mon grandpère, he was big man with temper, he was best kept out on the sea. He did better catching fish than tolerating people. Mon mére, your grandmère, she was fierce, big heart." His eyes teared. "She would have loved you so very hard... so very much."

His father had strong emotions and had no problem expressing them.

Zeus's blade began to spin again.

"If I knew you were growing in Zahira's womb, my face would've been the first you saw, my hands the first to hold you."

That strange feeling stirred inside Zeus's chest, and he looked behind him, down the hall to see if Sabrina was close.

"I didn't know," Sirius said. "I was never told of you until tonight. And for that, it is hard to forgive her. But I must, because here we are, together now. Father and son."

"She left me," he said, forgiveness wasn't really a thing in his world. "Days after I was born, she left me to live or die, I don't know which. I did a little of both until I left the orphanage for the streets of America."

"Thank you for surviving my son, thank you for this moment," Sirius said, pale eyes boring into Zeus', taking up space inside him.

"I often thought about the consequences of that one decision that changed all our futures," Sirius said. "But even now, I don't think I could have chosen different." He clenched and unclenched his large hands. "The last day I saw your mother, four older boys, French… maybe they grew tired of using words, wanted to hurt her physically. I was on my way to her when I heard the screams. I think you might know this feeling because I see how you are with your woman. I did not love your mother so deeply, but I was infatuated, and she'd just learned to smile. Who were they to take away her smile? To make her feel like her Algerian blood meant she wasn't entitled to one." He shrugged. "In many ways, I am my grandfather and the son of a butcher. Two died by my hands before the police come. Half my life I lived caged. Because of who they were, I receive longer time, despite that I acted in defense. I never saw your mother again after that day."

"Until today."

Sirius nodded. "Until today when Nabeela called, telling me to come meet my son. Everything between my imprisonment and now, will need to come from Zahira. I will stay the night." He told Zeus. "I will stay until you tell me to leave. And do not worry, I am good at cleaning blood."

"I'm good at making people bleed, so we work," Zeus said.

He stood and removed the mattress from the sofa bed, folded the frame back into the couch, and made up the mattress on the floor. "Sleeps better this way."

"To have this moment, to have new family, I would endure many more years of imprisonment... so you would live free. So, if blood needs to spill, I gladly return to place I spend half my life."

Zeus stood awkwardly, not knowing how to respond. If he had been placed in a caged like his father... either he would have been destroyed or the cage would have.

"I'm gonna make sure everything's secure. Tomorrow's movie night. But during the day..."

"Will there be popcorn? I like cheese flavored. Best kind."

Zeus grunted and walked out the back door. He didn't want to tell his father what would follow movie night, didn't want to involve him, jeopardize his freedom.

Standing alone in the night, he took a deep breath and looked up. The large blue-white dog star reminded him that his father had always been there, in his celestial form, looking down on him.

Shifting his attention from the heavens to the yard, he sensed something... off. Like an echo of something that had been there but wasn't there now.

Wasn't Aahod he was sensing, energy was different. It didn't take long to track the disturbance. Something pale fluttered on top of the retaining wall overlooking the canyon. He sensed that he was still alone, but his blades were out as he followed the sound and scent on the breeze.

At the retaining wall he leaned over and looked down into the cauldron of darkness below. He saw nothing, sensed nothing, and directed his attention to the stone on top of the wall weighing down a sheet of paper and something beneath it.

Walking the items back to the light he read the sliver of paper that simply stated: *You were too kind*.

Beneath the note was a photo of the remains of the assassin strewn over and around the bed on Kragen's yacht. *More are coming*, was written on the back of the photo.

Entering the shed, he opened the trap door and secured it behind him as he walked down the stairs that led to the earthen tunnel connecting the shed to the houses hidden cellar. Walking through pitch black, he stopped, years of practice led to instinct, and he quickly unbolted the locked door and stepped into work space that only he – and now Sabrina, Bri, and Sirius – knew about.

Retrieving his infrared night-vision goggles, he returned the way he had come stepped back over to the retaining wall and scoped the area behind the wall again. He confirmed what his senses told him, no one hid there, but a path of faint heat signatures remained. To climb the sheer cliff, the person who left the warning had to have been an elite climber.

Returning to the shed, he took a few traps out and reinstated them before walking the neighbors' yards, hunting for any remaining threats but not finding any. Heading back to the house he entered from the back door, softly locking it when he saw his father sleeping on the mattress.

Pulling his phone from his back pocket, there was only one number he needed to call to get answers.

"City Morgue. You kill 'em, we chill 'em."

The side of his mouth ticked up.

She wasn't his mother, not by blood or choice, but he could imagine her in the role more the woman he'd met earlier.

"I said no Brood, you promised me."

"Of course I did," he could hear the smile in Mama's voice.

"And I kept that promise. All my Brood, other than you, and Big Country are stateside. How are our girls? Did you meet your mother? Bring me something good back from France; I haven't been in ages."

Zeus rubbed the phone against his forehead and closed his eyes.

"He's not Brood," Terry said, from the background. "He's worse. A psychopath. You should always pick through Almaya's words before taking them at face value."

"Before you start throwing out labels and making judgments," Mama snapped. "Maybe you should remember that not even three months ago Zeus could've been viewed the same, and look at him now. When will you trust that I recognize my own?"

The two went back and forth, and after learning some of Zahira and Sirius' history, Zeus was curious about Mama and Terry's.

"Who's here?" He interrupted.

"Carl," Mama said. "He won't intrude on your time with Sabrina, he's only there as back up."

Zeus took a pic of the items Carl had left on his retaining wall and sent it using the Brood's encrypted messaging system.

"He needs to get farther fucking back," Zeus said. "He's too messy, destroyed my kind act."

"Yes, he did," Mama said softly, releasing a long stream of air.

"Who's the dead man?" Terry asked, closer to the phone.

"Confirmation that your long game is working. Kragen didn't hire an army to come after me and Sabrina because he doesn't have the money to fund one. The shark chum on the photo was Aahod, Basir's assassin, and Kragen had to call in a favor for that. Kragen the son being found decapitated on an estate where human trafficking occurred, and later being linked to the rapes and murders of a number of Black women, led Basir to apologize by offering Aahod."

Silence from the other side of the line, then....

"Well damn son, do I have to fear you coming for my job now?"

"Hell no."

Tonight, he saw that when given the opportunity to live, people would talk to save themselves. He'd never intentionally extended that opportunity before, but fathers had to listen and give corrective action. Aahod was a chance to practice. Carl ruined the outcome.

"Note says more are coming, so tomorrow night I'll hunt before they do."

"Do you need a safe hunting ground?" Mama asked.

Zeus smiled. "Got one."

"I'll send Carl to cover the house while you're away. He'll protect Sabrina and Bri."

"Why send him here in the first place? Why not send him after Kragen instead, since he's vulnerable?"

Silence.

"What Almaya sometimes forgets is that the Brood defends and protects. Ourselves and others," Terry said. "We have eaten the whale bit by bit and the Consortium is a dying entity. Kragen made no direct strike against us−"

"Until now," Mama said. "So *now*, you hunt," she told Zeus, flatly. "Carl has slept inside the Consortium, feeding us information for years. He's in Europe and I promised no Brood. Now that he's killed again, I doubt that he'll go back."

"We need to talk," Terry told Almaya. He was pissed. Him

and Mama were about to have conflict and Zeus didn't want to be on the line when they did.

"Make sure Carl stays on the house," Zeus said. "Between him and my father, Sabrina and Bri should be safe while I'm gone."

"Wait, your father! Back up! When—"

He disconnected the call.

Mama would call Sabrina to get the details in the morning, this he knew. They were always sharing details, always... talking.

"Is good?" His father asked.

He turned to see Sirius watching him.

Zeus handed him the photo and note. "How many blades you got?"

CHAPTER EIGHT

"I know my darling, but what can one expect?" Kragen said patiently as his wife vented her frustration.

"Perhaps now you'll seriously think about relocating to the house in Maine. No, it's not that we would be running from rumors, but the seclusion and privacy will allow us to focus on our remaining family while distancing ourselves from some of our less than stellar business associates in the Consortium. When push comes to shove, my love, we must protect ourselves above all others."

Exiting the rental car, Max stepped out into the cool night and walked until he reached the slip where one of the Consortium's midsized yachts was docked. The sound of lapping water and distant thumping, like a piece of wood hitting a metal tub, beat out like a Viking funeral dirge that paid homage to the son he was here to avenge.

"How soon will this be over, Max? All the lies, the seizures of our funds and properties. They are making us out to be criminals by association!"

"Soon, my darling. Trust me. Trust me to protect what remains of our family. I'll call you tomorrow after I set sail with the child."

"Everything will be ready when you return, be careful."

Max disconnected the call and walked towards the remote area where his yacht was docked. His two-man crew wasn't visible above deck as approached. In truth it looked like no preparations to ready the vessel for his arrival had been made though he'd been in conversation with the captain not even three hours ago.

He was normally a patient man, but the dereliction of duty in those he'd newly hired was intolerable. Basir's man was a prime example. Aahod had yet to contact Max and confirm that he'd secured the child, and with each moment that passed in silence, he found himself doing the unthinkable, second guessing himself. Perhaps he should not have trusted Basir, but he'd been desperate. If Basir had taken the child as he'd taken...

Max took a deep breath.

If Basir didn't keep his word, Maxim would simply use the Good Shepherd's men to kill both Zeus and Aahod. And Basir, his life would be forfeit. He would just consider it the price Basir needed to pay for allowing his son to be murdered inside his home.

Climbing aboard the sleek yellow and white sailing vessel, Maxim was non-plussed. It was as if he'd stepped inside a pressurized bubble. There was both an absence of sound and an absence of light except a dim glow below decks. Time seemed to slow, though his heart accelerated at an alarming rate.

He stepped quietly and precisely, knowing he had no weapons. Why would he need them? He was not a criminal.

But this was a Consortium vessel, there would be weapons below deck.

Max swallowed, tentatively stepping down the short flight of stairs. Pausing at the bottom step, he crouched a bit, and scanned the deeply shadowed lounge which was only illuminated by the moon and distant lights from the other ships.

He struggled to make sense of what he could only assume was blood. And he assumed, because he refused to turn on the lights and make himself a glaring target.

What the bloody hell had happened here?

It was if a large long-haired dog had stood in the center of the area rug and shook, sending droplets of blood to cover the polished teak table inlaid with gold, the couch facing the stars and the two love seats on either side of the couch forming a u-shaped seating area. The wet bar to the right of the stairs seemed to have chunks of... *flesh?*

He grimaced, not wanting to contemplate it, but he had to face it. The lockbox was in the wall behind the bar. Tipping towards it he used his key and opened it, pulling out a flare gun. It wasn't much as weapons went, but if the bloody beast was still on board, he had to protect himself, at the very least gravely injure it, because there would be no going to the police. The very last thing he needed was for the police to show up now.

He had to get this mess cleaned up before daylight, but the most he'd ever cleaned was money. Where the hell was his crew? Who had let this happen, and more importantly, who was responsible?

Something heavy hit the deck above and he flinched – an instinctive reaction that he was grateful no one saw. He crouched behind the bar.

Footsteps moved above, heavy, unconcerned about whether they alerted others to their presence.

It was certainly not Aahod. He was stealthy.

Max's hand shook as he wrestled with fear. He was stuck between simply staying hidden, or aiming the gun in the direction of the stairs.

He hadn't been in this position of needing to defend himself since he was a child. He usually had a wall of protection, but all around him those walls had been crumbling. He'd never missed their presence as profoundly as he did in this moment.

"So, do we even know if he's here, like?" An Irish voice called out.

"Be vigilant little brother, be disciplined, you will not survive if patience does not guide your head in the world as it does at the Keep."

Maxim's whole body sagged, his terror a cage that dematerialized the moment it was clear that it was the Shepherd's men who approached.

Placing the flare gun behind him, he stood and assumed an unaffected demeanor, inwardly seething over the situations his son was *still* able to place him in. If not for this obligation to his son, he would be home with his wife focused on rebuilding the reputation of the Consortium and shoring up the legacy of the dynasty he'd created. And that would begin with dismantling this organization known as Mama's Brood. Starting with Zeus.

Six men filled the lounge. Each one was dressed in robes, cowls, and roped belts. Though there was a variety of shapes and sizes among the men, there was only one color, the color of efficiency.

"I am so pleased you are here," Max said.

"Bloody hell man, did you slaughter the pig and cow on your own then?" The young Irishman asked as he looked around the blood splattered room. He was the slenderest of the group, and one could practically smell the mother's milk on his breath.

"I do not kill," Max corrected. "I was in the process of investigating when you arrived."

"And did you find the killer behind the fecking bar then?" the younger man laughed. "Or did ya shite yourself thinking you were next?"

The sternest looking man in the group backhanded the younger. The brutality of the strike made him stumble back and fall, quickly finding his feet and holding himself in rigid respect.

"Forgive me brother," he said, eyes straight ahead, his prior animation reduced to a deadpan monotone.

"You're Kragen?" The stern one asked.

Of the six he appeared to be the oldest and the most similar to the Good Shepherd in demeanor.

"I am," Max confirmed. "I haven't located the two crewmen who are supposed to be here, but I'm one hundred percent sure the man you were sent to... purify, has done this."

The Brother looked at him long and hard before nodding towards the others.

Two of the men walked up the stairs returning to the upper deck and two moved deeper into the room towards the closed bedroom doors.

"I am Gideon, and this is Neri," he said, indicating the young one beside him. He nodded towards the two men moving towards the door.

Neither seem prepared to face someone capable of slaughter, approaching the door as they did, carelessly with no weapons or commitment to attacking or defending themselves.

"That is Jacob," Gideon said of the dark haired one on the right. "And that is Adriel," he said, pointing towards the ginger haired man on the left.

"Brothers Abel and Peter will ensure that no one else comes onto the boat."

Boat. It was a fucking million-dollar yacht.

The Brothers opened the double doors to the bedroom suite and one, he couldn't see which, inhaled sharply. Neither entered the room.

If Gideon and Neri weren't obstructing the path between where Max stood and the stairs, he would've moved with determination to the upper level. It was bad enough here, he dreaded what awaited in the bedroom.

To avoid being perceived as a coward, Max moved towards the bedroom when Gideon motioned for him to do so. He was at least emboldened by the belief that the killer couldn't be in there because the first pair of Brothers were inside.

Gideon and Neri followed him with measured steps.

When Max saw the display before him, the savagery of it, the gruesome artistry, he couldn't help but feel a thrill. He would not become a victim tonight, but Aahod definitely had.

Basir's little assassin had failed.

Miserably.

His remains desecrated the bed and floor. Maxim had intended to sleep here tonight; now that would not be possible.

It was unfortunate Zeus had murdered his son; if they had met under different circumstances, he would've gladly recruited him as a member into the Consortium's rank of enforcers.

"There's no one above," one of the men who'd gone top deck said from behind, startling Max. "Living or dead."

"We will cleanse the space," Gideon said. "Do you have someplace else to stay until tomorrow night?"

"Of course," Max said, relieved to relinquish responsibility to the Shepherd's men and make his way to the stairs. He paused before walking up them.

"Will you be able to match this level of violence?" he asked Gideon.

"No. We will surpass it."

He smiled as he left the yacht and alerted the driving service that he would need to return to the Consortium's chateau a few miles away.

Once he was comfortably embedded in the car, he smiled as he hit Basir's contact information.

He was going to enjoy telling the bastard that his *revered* assassin died in utter failure. Perhaps Basir would now understand the humiliation of losing someone to such hateful violence. And because Max had the Good Shepherd's strength behind him, he no longer needed to kowtow to Basir for support.

Actually, he thought, hearing the other man pick up the line, when fate eventually led the authorities to Basir's door, he would know what it meant to no longer have Max as a valued asset. And then... then Max would finally be able to reclaim what Basir took from him all those years ago.

CHAPTER NINE

"Okay Zuki," Sabrina said, lying naked on the bed. "If your daddy isn't here in five minutes, we gotta get up and go get him. This goes beyond protection. He's fixating."

Zeus's compulsive need to care for them was in overdrive.

Sabrina's own protective instincts grew tenfold the moment she'd learned of Bri's existence, and now that she had a little zygote developing in her womb, she would kill without remorse to protect them. But Zeus... he couldn't keep this up. He was not a machine that could exist without rest, he wasn't an invincible God, it was just getting him to believe that.

"Maybe he'll be better by the time you're born," she told Zuki. "Actually, he'll probably be worse; yeah, let's assume he'll be worse."

But he had her to watch over him now, it wasn't like when he was a boy living inside the hell of that orphanage. The thought of him isolated in that room with only a devil mask to interact with made her want to snap necks.

"The fucking cruelty of it all Zuki, is just–"

The bedroom door opened, and Zeus stepped into the room, knives out. His eyes flicked over her naked body before slowly scanning the space.

"Who were you talking to?" he asked, his intent to commit violence obvious, but as he let the door click shut, so was something else.

He really is a beautiful man. Beautiful and deadly and complex, and −

His penetrating look demanded a response.

"I'm talking to Zuki," she sighed.

He looked around the room again and that fucking attitudinal eyebrow rose high when his gaze settled back on her.

"So, this Zuki a spirit, because we are the only ones in the room?"

This from a man who had conversations with his blades like they were sentient beings, which, at this point, she kind of believed they were.

"Zuki, instead of Godzuki," she pointed at her stomach. "We're bonding."

He frowned at her, processing, then placed his blades on the dresser, crawled onto the bed, and stretched out beside her, his head resting against one hip as he draped his arm over her pelvis and stroked the side of her stomach with his thumb.

"Whatever she said is probably wrong," he spoke against her stomach and kissed it gently. "She's overly emotional and extremely illogical," Zeus continued.

She popped him on the head, then bent down to kiss the spot she'd abused, and lay her arm over his shoulder, stroking the hard muscle encased in soft skin.

He lifted his head and looked down at her stomach, as if staring Zuki in its yet unformed eyes. "See what I mean?"

"For your information," Sabrina laughed, "I was telling Zuki that you are the best protector a family could have."

He squinted at her, and it was her turn to arch a brow and cock her head and he settled back against her stomach. "Okay she's right. But come to me for verification on the important stuff; like blades and spirits and hunting and your demi-god powers."

Lord, this poor child.

She stayed quiet as Zeus told Zuki their story, the story of how they'd met, and it was filled with–

"Lies!" she shrieked again, laughing so hard she was too weak to push him off her.

He watched until her laughter settled into a soft smile. "I'm funny as shit," he told her stomach.

Oh my God, was he seriously offended that people didn't always find his humor funny?

"I. Am. Funny. As. Shit."

"Ok, you know what–"

"And it's not lies, it's perspective. She has none." He told Zuki.

"So, you laying on your ass, watching rugby while I broke my back cleaning your dirty assed cabin was a matter of perspective?"

"Yep. 'Cause from my perspective, what you did wasn't cleaning."

Oh hell no!

She tried to wrestle him off her but when he wrapped his arms around her hips he was like a barnacle and wouldn't let go.

Out of breath, she flopped back onto the bed.

"Just like I wouldn't call a yard squirrel a monster," he drawled, derisively.

Now it was a simple matter of pride.

She tried to roll off the bed and take him with her, hoping to at least land on top and pin him down.

It was futile. Nothing worked. He was a strong immovable force, and she was *tired*.

They settled into silence, him rubbing her stomach, and her stroking his head.

"You were gone a while; you ready to tell me what happened?"

"Why are you calling my Godzuki, Zuki?"

He'd tell her what happened, she already knew that, but she also knew that when Zeus wanted a question answered, he'd focus on getting it answered before he moved on.

"Godzuki was Godzilla's *son*. Zuki is little now, still forming, still determining what it will be. I want it to choose, without us influencing what it'll be."

"Okay," he told her stomach. "Sometimes she makes sense. Her woman's brain is unpredictable that way, it'll keep you on your toes. Maybe one day she'll use it to become a better fighter, but one day is not today."

She refrained from bopping him on the head again.

Maybe she wasn't the best with blades, but she was a damn good fighter; he just didn't want to admit it.

Reaching into his back pocket, Zeus pulled out what Sabrina thought were two pieces of paper, and handed them to her.

"Mama sent someone to watch our backs. Someone not Brood. So technically she didn't break her promise."

That was the thing with Almaya, she generally kept he word, but you had to pay attention to what *wasn't* said as much as what was.

"Can't say I'm mad about it," Sabrina muttered after reading, *You were too kind.*

More are coming, was written on the second.

She frowned and flipped it over. She couldn't stop her reaction to the gore captured on the photo.

"What the fuck is this?"

"Not Brood," Zeus said, hand sliding up to her breast. "But Mama's none-the-less." He stated the words as if reciting them.

Sabrina tried not to judge, but sometimes....

When Zeus killed those men in the warehouse in under two minutes, it was her first encounter with him. Beautiful and terrifying.

This was just terrifying.

"Almaya trusts him?"

Zeus shifted higher up on her body, resting his head closer to her breast.

He wasn't slick.

"Terry doesn't," he said, kissing the side of her breast. "But Almaya sees things in people. Beyond the violence. Think she's part witch."

More like all witch.

His hand slid towards her inner thigh.

Okay, he was a little slick.

"If someone showed me a picture of that warehouse floor after you'd killed those men, I would've had the same reaction," she said, her voice huskier than it was a minute ago.

"That's because you don't know how to see. I left Aahod on Kragen's yacht wounded, but alive. It was a teaching moment," he said.

He flicked her nipple. "But Carl – that's the someone not

Brood guy – Carl didn't give Aahod a chance to learn the lesson."

"And what was the lesson?"

"That if they want to continue living, they'll stay the fuck away. With him dead they won't get the message."

She looked at the picture again. "Oh, I think they'll get it."

"He's a good killer, but dramatic," he said, skimming a finger just inside her lower lips, already slick with arousal. "He's good at slipping in and out unnoticed. He left those without me sensing him, but he knew not to approach the house."

"Do you trust him to have your back?"

He shrugged. "I trust Mama. Carl said more are coming, so I stop them before they do. You cleaning other people's blood from places we live, that's gotta end. So I end it. Sirius will also stay while I'm hunting."

"I'm glad Sirius is staying, he's a sweet man. But let's be clear Zeus; when you're gone, I'm responsible for my family. I fight for my family. And I'm happy that family now includes Sirius. Do you know he showed me how to get rid of blood like three different ways? Meat tenderizer. Who would've known you could clean away blood with meat tenderizer?"

"You would've known if you learned to cook." He rolled off the bed before she could land more than one blow. "This violence of yours doesn't set a good example for Zuki," he criticized, as he walked around the room, laying his blades to rest for the night. He removed his clothes and stared down at her instead of getting back in bed, probably determining if it was safe. Like she was the blade wielding killer in the family.

"You've got a lot of nerve–"

"I got a lot of other stuff too." He said, glancing down at

his dick before his dancing silver eyes and half smile landed back on her

"Uhn uh," she said, turning on her side, and tucking one arm around her pillow, ignoring the blade hidden there as she smiled knowingly at him. She waved her other hand at his dick. "I'm too tired for all that."

She faked a yawned for effect.

Despite her words, she ate him up with her eyes, limb by limb, piece by piece. His dark golden skin glowed with health, and she wondered if licked, would he be salty, sweet, or savory. No matter what flavor he was, he was all times delicious.

"You're too tired," Zeus reflected, staring at the blank wall as he weighed her words and his perceptions. Then his gaze nailed her against the bed. Her pussy clenched. He looked down at his body, rubbing a hand over his chest and abs. He reached down and stroked a hand back and forth along his long thick erection.

"Too tired for all this," he said, as if he felt sorry for her.

She knew he was fucking with her but when the side of his mouth inched up, she determined it was *on*. And she wasn't going to be the one to give in.

Shifting onto her back, she stroked her hand over her breasts then rubbed her stomach. "I have a whole being sucking from my body. I can be tired if I want to be tired."

"Be tired then," he said, and it grated because he sounded just like her.

She frowned as he walked across the room and turned off the ceiling light, plunging the room into darkness. She felt him climb into bed and just... lay there.

What the hell was he waiting for?

She drew closer, pressing her breast against his arm.

He reached over and patted the crown of her head like she was a dog.

"Let Zuki feed, you rest," he said. But it was the way he said it, it made her feel like he was offering her up to some vampire, zombie, alien parasite.

She shifted onto her back and gazed up at the dark ceiling. Was he fucking with her? Using new Jedi mind tricks he'd learned from Terry?

She rolled back towards him angled her leg over his thighs, rubbing her hand over his relaxed ab muscles.

"Doesn't feel like you're resting," he said.

"Touching you helps me feel restful."

A growl rumbled deep within his chest. She smiled in the dark. That sound meant he was tired of her bullshit. He obviously failed to realize where Bri got her bullshit drama gene.

"I like when you purr," she whispered. "I can feel it vibrate inside of me."

She lifted his hand and guided it between her thighs. "Right here", she said, pressing his index and pointer fingers into her opening of her, pushing their four fingers deep within, moving leisurely.

She shifted, covering more of his body with hers, moaning as she rested her head against his shoulder, his fingers moving independently within her now, pushing deeper and deeper, finding the spots that made her back arch, made her groan.

"Your resting seems a lot like our fucking," he said, grabbing her thigh and pulling her fully on top of him. She straddled wide, ass up as she pumped up and down on his hand. She placed her hands beside his shoulders, lifting her chest off him, giving him ample opportunity to–

He sucked a nipple into his mouth as if it were ripe fruit on a low-lying vine. The suction shot sensation straight to her pussy, which contracted hard around the pleasure, around his fingers, squeezing as if they could produce the liquid heat she wanted.

Zeus's mouth pulled away from her breast and his fingers stopped the delicious movement inside her.

She groaned and opened her eyes.

"So, you ready to sleep?" Zeus drawled, yawning loudly. It was a fake yawn, but he wasn't that good of an actor.

"I will bite you," she snapped, in frustration.

"Not the threat you think it is."

His dry tone exemplified how you laugh at someone without showing you're laughing at them.

Sabrina lowered her upper body onto his. Tucking her head in the crook of his neck, she gently bit, then licked the area.

His fingers, still inside, didn't move.

She bit again, harder, but not hard enough to break the skin.

Zeus grunted. His fingers twitched inside her before pulling them free of her body completely.

He moved, and the world spun. When she oriented herself, the side of her face was pressed into the pillow, and he held her head down with one hand as he adjusted her body to lie flatly on the bed beneath him. His erection weighed against the crease of her ass as he sat against the back of her thighs.

"So, we've made it to boss level three, see which player can withstand the highest level of pain. This should be fun."

Her heart pounded with fear and anticipation, she tried to push her head off the pillow.

It was a love bite. Why did he always have to take things to the outer fucking limit!?

His hand fisted in her hair, and he pulled her head back to within inches of his chest. His other hand gripped her throat, and he lowered his mouth to her ear.

"Don't resist, you'll only make it worse," Zeus warned, and instantly she was in a different room with a different man, at a different time, and she was fighting for her life.

I always love how you resisted, Kragen said. *Always. The harder you fought, the harder I took you.*

She had been fighting as much for her sister as she was for her own sanity, for her own body integrity. He couldn't win, she couldn't let him -

Weight and heat pressed her entire body so firmly into the mattress that she thought she'd be pushed through it.

She couldn't move, she had to move, she couldn't let him take her, break her, not when she'd–

"Who am I, Sabrina? Whose voice is in your ear?"

She blinked, surrounded by darkness. Where did the gold and white room go? Where did–

"Who is with you now? The one that needs you, that would give up his life so that you could live?"

"You," she sobbed, squeezing her eyes tight to fight the release of fresh tears.

"Who am I?"

"Zeus," she said, reaching for his hand beside hers. She laced her fingers through his and pressed her lips against his fingers.

He always held her down, and at times like this, he literally held her down, his body on top of hers, head resting against her head, legs stretched over her legs, arms curved to the exact angle of her arms.

"I'm sorry," she said, feeling ashamed. She'd survived so

much more than Kragen, *so much more*, yet her mind and body continued to betray her with those last moments with him, her *sister's* boogeyman, her *sister's* rapist, and despite how hard she fought, if Zeus hadn't shown up, he would've also been hers.

Zeus rubbed his nose against her ear.

"If you're ready to apologize for something, it should be for refusing to make the bed." Sabrina smiled and bit his knuckle. "Or for that. Never for him. Never for surviving." He kissed her damp cheek. "It's what we do. At all costs."

He shifted his weight off of her and lay his head on her pillow as she turned to face him. His mercurial eyes seemed to shine in the dark as he gazed at her intently.

"At all costs," she said, molding her fingers over the hard angles of his face. "But I'm telling you truthfully, from the deepest depths of my heart; I will never apologize for not making a stupid bed."

"Don't need your apologies. Just need you to be a responsible adult. Make the bed."

She laughed, leaned over, and kissed him.

Bless his heart, he knew as well as she did that that wasn't happening.

"See," he said, his voice deep, contemplative as he rubbed his thumb over her still smiling lips. "I'm funnier than you. It's true. You and Bri laugh at what I say, more than I laugh at what you say."

"That's because you're humorless."

"No, you're just not funny."

"Let this be your first lesson Zuki," he said, splaying his hand over her stomach. "Your father is funnier than your mother, but you'll have to laugh at her jokes so her little wounded feelings don't lead to violence."

"My *God*," she shrieked softly, pushing him onto his back and straddling him again.

"See what I mean?" he said, still talking to Zuki.

"It's because you drive me to it!" she hissed. She looked at her stomach. "I was a pacifist before–"

Zeus leaned forward and kissed her, before she could lie to their child.

"Who am I?" he asked, when she was soft and breathless.

"Zeus," she whispered. "Man I love. Father of a Kaiju."

He waited.

She groaned.

"A God."

"A God," he said, guiding her head down to rest against his shoulder. "Now go to sleep. We'll show Zuki how their father is the best lover you've ever had after you rest."

"No. We won't. Because that would be weird and inappropriate."

He was quiet for so long she'd slipped into the first stages of sleep.

"It already knows anyway," she heard, Zeus assure himself.

CHAPTER TEN

Gideon entered Kragen's suite, immediately clocking the fine china, the expensive upholstery, the marble, the gold. Just like the yacht, the excess, the gluttony, were on full display.

In another life this would've been his. Because he would have taken it. Cracked Kragen over the head and had a crew in and out of here in minutes. Now he dutifully walked across the room, stopping in front of the third-floor window overlooking a pool, tennis court, and beyond the trees and ten-foot wall, a golf course in the distance.

If the Shepherd was going to expand the flock's reach, this would be the perfect place.

"I assume everything has been taken care of?" Kragen asked on entering the room.

Gideon and the other priests had worked through the night and well into the morning, as this bough bag slept in the comforts of a warm bed and perfumed sheets. This was why the Good Shepherd's order was going to hold all the power once Kragen's husk of an organization burned itself out.

"Yes, the yacht is ready for your use."

"And the killer?"

"The killer...." Gideon said, watching a woman, skin the color of desert sand, hair heavy and black, stroll towards the pool in heels, her white, nearly nonexistent bikini blinding against her flesh. "That's why I've come. A message was left for you this morning, delivered by a street kid." He turned from the woman, reached into the pocket of his robe, and extracted the envelope. Although it was addressed to Kragen, he'd read it before coming.

It was the reason he had come.

He watched Kragen's reaction.

The killer's letter was abrupt.

I have what you want, but you'll only get it if I'm dead. I'm not dying, so let's talk.

There was an address and a time.

"Do you know this place?" Kragen asked.

Gideon nodded. "I made it a point to drive by it on my way here. It's an old convent, nearly abandoned. We'll have to alter your appearance, otherwise you'll stick out in that area of town. You won't want to be remembered there."

"You and your priests will take me to him?"

Gideon hesitated. There were other avenues to consider, but Kragen had taken the killer's bait.

"We will," he said, unwilling to discuss his additional plans. "But what outcome do you desire?"

"He and I will talk, then you will kill him. He will die screaming, and we will find the child. The plan has not changed."

Gideon lifted the cowl over his head.

"We will return and head to the location in two hours."

"A bit early, don't you think?" Kragen asked drolly.

"Are you suggesting we arrive fashionably late, or even on time, allowing the killer time to execute whatever plan he's making?"

This man was bloated with ignorance about how punishment truly worked. He was a cosplayer, playing at violence and power, but what power was there to be had when you practiced it against those unable to fight back.

There would be a real and significant change to the Consortium soon, one that would see a shift in power to the Shepherd's Keep.

"Well, when you put it like that, I think it be best to defer to your expertise."

"Indeed. Sir," Gideon said.

"Is it safe for me to return to the yacht now?"

"It's best that you remain here until we come for you. The killer doesn't know of this place, but he knows of the yacht. Let's not make this easy for him."

Gideon left the chateau uncertain whether it was poetic justice or divine intervention that led Zeus to choose the church as the place he'd receive final judgment. But no matter, he would contact the Good Shepherd and prepare the Brothers for the fight. And Zeus would die on sacred grounds so that his soul could quickly find its final resting place in hell.

Sabrina's stomach chased itself in sickening circles as she stood next to the SUV.

She should let him go.

It was getting dark, and he needed to go, but she didn't want to let him.

Today had been the perfect day, he had given them that, and all she wanted to do was have a perfect night of holding him, holding them all – Zeus, Bri, Sirius – to her and know that they would be safe.

"It feels different." She needed him to understand. "I know you can withstand unbelievable pain and do things that sometimes defy logic. I *know* your Blade Spirits protect you Zeus, but this feels different. Something feels wrong, in my gut, in my spirit, something feels wrong."

He wouldn't look at her, continued gazing at the house where Sirius and Briana stood inside the doorway. "At least take Si–"

"No."

She took a deep breath, ready to jump in the back seat.

This was insane!

As if he could hear her internal ranting, his steely gaze flickered towards her.

"This is what I do, it's who I am. Before you. Before the Brood. But *us*... makes me... more. I know what it feels like to be loved. I'm not letting that go. I'll be back. But if I'm near death what will you do?"

"Call on the Blade Spirits and a doctor?" He snorted and she smiled. "And if I get lost in the darkness?"

"I'll step into it and drag your ass back out. Fight your demons just like you help me fight mine.

"Maybe not just like. I'm a much better fighter."

"You're an idiot."

"That you love."

"That I absolutely love. With all my heart."

He started the engine, shifting uncomfortably in his seat.

"I feel heavy," he said, grimacing. "Weighed down."

Because she'd made him wear the protective gear Almaya sent in her care package. Him wearing it was non-negotiable. "You'll be fine, you're doing this for me remember?"

He grunted. "Use the program Mama sent. If the perimeter is breached, go to the cellar; there's enough for all three of you to survive down there for a month if needed. And if you need to fight your way out... you know where the weapons are."

"Plan for all the eventualities you can," she said, reciting one of his many lessons. "But we'll be fine. You just do the same, because you got a whole Zuki waiting for another blade lullaby".

That half smile made her knees week.

"I've got a whole lot more waiting for me," he said, looking at Bri and Sirius.

Without another word, he reached out and brought her face within millimeters of his. "We are bound. Protecting each other in this live and the next."

His kiss was brief, but she could feel it all the way down to the arch of her feet.

She watched the SUV role backwards out of the drive, the fence shutting again as he left the safety of their home.

In their time together, this was the first time he'd left her alone with anyone other than the Brood. As much as he disrespected her abilities, he trusted her. Not only Sirius, not only Carl, but her. He trusted her to keep their family safe.

And she would. She would also protect him.

Pulling her phone from her pocket she went to favorites and pressed.

The phone rang twice.

"How's it going?"

"Zeus just left. I want you to do me a favor."

Mama listened without interruption.

"He won't like it," she said, when Sabrina finished.

"And that's okay, I've had to deal with a lot more than him not liking something. If it gets him back home safe, I'll deal with his anger."

"Okay. Where he's going?"

"The old convent. The one where he was raised."

"I'll make the call, but I honestly don't know how this'll play out Sabrina. He's very unpredictable."

"Understood," she said walking back to the house. "But if nothing else, this relationship has taught me the lengths I'll go to protect what remains of my family."

"Now you've played around and unlocked Mama Bear level of existence. You now have the ability to understand why I do what I do."

Sabrina laughed. "Sorry Mama, but I don't ever want to understand why you do what you do."

"It's called raise heaven and earth levels of destruction on any motherfucker who tries it. Don't worry dear, you'll get there," Almaya said, hanging up.

When Sabrina reached the front door, she kneeled down to Briana's level and saw the glint of a large blade held behind Sirius's thigh.

She smiled up at him with gratitude.

He'd taken to his role as grandfather and father instantly, adding a prized piece to their familial puzzle; locking into place as if he'd been waiting a lifetime to fill the space.

"Alright, Little Bit, you got everything you need?"

Briana nodded and held up two fingers.

"This is the *second* night–"

Sabrina circled those two fingers within her fist and kissed the tips. "Don't start little girl. Today was fun and play, tonight we got jobs to do, and while Zeus is away doing his part, we have to do ours."

"When am I going to be old enough for guard duty?" Briana asked.

"Zeus is the one who trains you, you'll have to ask him."

Sabrina had no problem throwing Zeus under the bus because if she had her way, Bri would never be old enough.

Briana smirked and nodded. "It'll be soon then."

Sabrina directed Bri inside the house and Sirius shut the door behind them.

Bri's confidence came from believing she could get Zeus to do anything if she asked nicely enough. With just about anything else, Sabrina may have been concerned, but Zeus wasn't going to put Bri in harm's way until he believed she could take care of herself.

Which would probably be never.

"Okay, the number one rule for tonight?" she asked Bri as they moved towards the cellar entrance Bri had learned about earlier that day.

"Don't make a sound," Bri said.

Sabrina nodded.

"I guard house," Sirius said. "Only way in is through me."

Sirius had wanted to fight alongside Zeus. She'd listened as he'd tried to make his case, but she could've told him it was useless.

"If they're not safe...."

That's all Zeus said, and Sirius understood the honor he was being given.

"I'll make sure the cameras are on," Sabrina said.

She opened the hidden wall panel and walked down the steps behind Bri.

Zeus had cleared a space and put down a pallet with all the things that usually kept Bri's attention: iPad, books, art supplies, and food. There was a compost toilet against one wall and blades all around, some still in the process of being made.

"Rule number two: don't touch a single blade in here except the one in your backpack. Do *not*," she emphasized. "And you know Zeus will be able to tell. And neither he nor I will be happy, like automatic punishment for the rest of your life unhappy."

Briana sat on the pallet and reached for her iPad and earbuds.

There was a refrigerator, a generator, food, and water, plus the laptop Mama sent that now monitored every entry point of the house, as well as views of the front and back yards. Mama guessed that Zeus had a basic assed security system, and she was right. Looking around the space, Sabrina had a feeling Zeus spent more time down here than any other part of the house.

"I'll be back in a couple hours. Text me only if it's important."

"*Yes!* He downloaded the *His Dark Materials* series! Mrs. Jace wouldn't let me watch it because it's PG13 but I—"

Her eyes wide and she went silent as she realized she may have said too much.

"*I'm* the one who downloaded it, thank you very much," Sabrina corrected. "But I've seen what you read, Ms. Active Imagination. It'll be fine."

Briana placed the iPad beside her and stood as Sabrina headed back up the stairs.

"I thought you were supposed to stay down here with me."

"I'll be down soon. Girls' secret, Sirius is tough, but I don't want him up there alone. This cellar is a hidden fortress. You'll be the safest, which is as it should be." She bent down and kissed the crown of Bri's head.

"I'll be back before the third episode. And I'll bring down a special treat for being good at following the rules."

After securing the cellar, she walked to the front door and looked out.

"You're supposed to be below," Sirius said behind her.

She turned and smiled, tapping her temple. "Woman's brain. Frustrates the hell out of your son but you seem more like a roll with it kind of guy."

His electric pale eyes sparkled with humor. "Definitely a 'roll with it' guy," he said. His accented voice could go from teasing and affectionate to unyielding in seconds.

"Why haven't you married, Sirius? Are you still in love with Zahira?"

"I love life." Yeah, she got a sense that meant women loved *him*. He had that kind of magnetism. "Will settle for nothing less than what you have with my son."

She looked towards the gate anxiously hoping his son would drive back through it soon. It didn't matter that he'd just left.

"Let's lock it down," she sighed.

He grunted. "Stay safe. And if we must, make enemy sorry."

"Exactly."

CHAPTER ELEVEN

Zeus walked onto the church grounds ignoring the sounds that floated into the courtyard from the street: French hip hop, shrill laughter, traffic, arguing. The courtyard itself was empty, which meant Jean-Pierre had done his job.

Death is coming, Zeus had told him, *the only ones who should be here are those ready to die.*

The child's non-judgmental eyes sparked with satisfaction when Zeus passed him another five-hundred euros. It took a lot to survive on the streets, even when you had family. The odd jobs meant JP and his family didn't have to worry about him being arrested or taken away anymore. Tonight, he'd asked JP to talk to his parents about renting his house for less money and more space than they would get in the city. After this trip Zeus wouldn't really need this property anymore. He was settling down. Plus, he had other properties.

And a family.

Veering towards the old hospital, Zeus pulled a board off

one of the windows and crept into the building, walked through the nearly black halls cleaned of everything but the graffiti covering the walls, ground, and ceiling. He made his way to the section of the hospital where the power was still active and florescent lights flicked on and off, as if trapped between life and death with no clear way out of this purgatory.

Just like at the church and orphanage, bad things happened in the hospital but not as bad because the clergy had to be mindful of the regular staff that worked here. The same staff allowed him to help out because, despite the nun's interventions, aka beatings, they couldn't force him to stay away. It was mostly because of the babies. He liked sneaking in to see the mothers with their babies, liked to pretend.... He grunted, turned off the main hall and headed towards the surgery unit.

He would have his own baby soon, and it would be like the lucky ones, the ones that got to leave.

Pushing through the swinging doors of the surgery unit, Zeus walked to the built-in cabinet where one of the doors hung at an angel, removed the false bottom, and pulled out and old scalpel that saved his life once. It wasn't one of his, it'd belonged to the surgical team but he kept it, made sure it didn't rust or show the same signs of deterioration that every-thing else here experienced.

Unlike the two Kusarigama attached to the back of the bullet proof vest, the bowies, and the throwing knives, he would coat the scalpel with the paralytic Mama sent in her care package. He couldn't desecrate his own blades that way. Covering the scalpel's blade with a hard plastic casing, he placed it inside a fleshy prosthetic adhesion attached to his forearm and sealed it, hiding it away like so many of his other blades. As he left the building, he periodically rotated his wrist, testing the adhesion.

The poison was supposed to incapacitate his opponents, so he could interrogate them quickly. For some reason Mama wanted Kragen alive, but Zeus had no interest in asking why.

Climbing the rarely used stairwell at the back of the church, he moved along the second story corridor towards the choir loft overlooking sanctuary and rows of pews filling the nave.

They were here.

He couldn't see them, but he sensed them inside the church, posted in the shadows, hiding, waiting. For him.

He smiled, watching the light from a hundred candles make the shadows danced almost ecstatically at the front of the church. The scent of mold sat upon the pews like parishioners. Of the few straggling visitors, only the most desperate remained, maybe hoping to have a roof to sleep under tonight.

This was the face of St. Catherine's now, sagging and hollow and desperate, filled with things, unsightly things, that moved behind its stained glassy eyes.

More than ever before seeing it in this state felt like retribution.

He had a family, and the diocese had... this.

A few priests entered the space below and began escorting the staunchest believers, or the most repentant sinners, towards the wood and metal doors. When all the parishioners were gone, one of the cowled priests sat at the front pew as the others, the ones that were too sure footed, too efficient, faded back into the shadows. Zeus wondered what happened to the bent and broken Father Garity, the man that watched over the bones of this place for the last five years.

The man sitting at the front of the church crossed his leg at the knee, exposing expensive black shoes that reflected the red glow of the flames.

Not a priest, not a killer, but the man that placed the kill order.

"Kragen-the-father," Zeus said, his words barely a whisper but loud enough to float gently on the air.

The man tensed, but the echo of Zeus's voice made it impossible to determine his location right away.

He could kill Kragen. Right now. Put a blade through his third eye, blind him from seeing what would come for him in hell.

"And you must be Zeus, the man who murdered my son," Kragen said, searching.

"Nah," Zeus said, donning his devil mask, making himself visible before slipping back into the shadows.

He was more than Kragen-the-son's killer, but he wasn't stupid enough to share his identity to anyone listening or recording the exchange. He wouldn't be caged or caught for protecting his heart.

Shifting, he moved from the area. If Kragen's men were as skilled as he believed, someone was already heading in his direction.

Climbing down to the ground level, he waited as one of the cloaked men moved passed. Stepping behind the priest, Zeus covered his mouth, and put him in a chokehold, constricting his arm muscles firmly around the throat of the other man as he fought to free himself. Which he eventually did once his body relaxed and sagged towards the ground.

Zeus dragged the unconscious man to a curtained alcove and placed him inside, pulling the curtain closed behind him.

Moving down the back hall he'd earlier walked with

Sabrina and Bri, he scanned the area, before taking the bait and stepping out onto the raised platform of the sanctuary. Kragen startled when he saw how close Zeus was, his eyes flicked to the scalpel now in Zeus's hand, then scanned the church, expecting to be saved.

"You should've grieved the dead son and let him burn in peace. But here you are, sacrificing yourself for a dead motherfucker who deserved worse than they got."

"I want my grandchild?"

The blades vibrated all over Zeus's body, making it a tuning fork that began to shake free the darkness inside.

The side of his mouth shifted upwards, but his head dipped low and tilted to the side.

"*You* want?"

"I do. And I *will* have."

Something whistled in the air to his left, Zeus shifted and heard the projectile thump against the wall behind him before falling to the ground.

Not a blade, not metallic, but something with weight.

Another came, then another, and this time he didn't move fast enough to avoid the two bolas from wrapping around his legs, another wrapped around his torso, pinning his arms to his sides as he toppled to the ground, landing hard on the dusty floor.

Four priests converged swiftly, and he couldn't stop the blows, one after the other. They performed their violence in grunts and silence as Kragen sat like a king, watching with pleasure.

"As I said, I will have the child, and the woman you saved," he shook his head in fake pity. "But what you saved her from then will be worse than either of you ever imagined. She will beg for death, and just when she believes her wish has been granted, she will beg some more. And through it all, the child will watch, knowing that if she ever displeases me, such a fate just may be her own." Kragen stood. "It's necessary you see, to rule children through fear."

A foot slammed into Zeus's face, and the devil mask crunched.

No one pulled guns or knives, but in synchronicity, the four men reached into their robes and pulled wooden rods half the length their bodies, and proceeded to pummel him.

The blades and vest beneath his clothing absorbed most of the impact, but each blow shrunk the chasm between the present and the past, transporting Zeus back to the isolation room, back to priests attempting to beat the devil out of him... for the third straight day.

Huddled in a corner, bruised, and swollen, he watched as the priest entered the isolation room that final day. He'd claimed his only wish to was to save Zeus's soul, but even Zeus knew that the man didn't care whether Zeus embraced God by way of life or by way of death.

What Zeus ended up embracing was his true saviors, the ones that called to him when the pain tempted him to give up, give in, to lose himself. He ended up embracing the ones that promised to protect him, to save him, to help him take away the pain. Those voices didn't try to change him. They accepted him, promised to stay devoted to him....

"You will yield, or you will break, boy?" the sweating priest shouted, breathing heavily as he lifted the rod again. "The choice is yours."

The choice is yours, the spirits echoed.

Yes. The choice was his.

And the moment he made it, the pain abated, his mind sharpened, and he kicked out at the priest's wooden rod mid descent, snapping it in half. Catching the falling half, Zeus crouched and lunged, ramming the jagged broken edge deep into the priest's gut.

The unrobed man fell to his knees clutching his midsection and Zeus stuck the bloody edge into the priest's chest.

The isolation room transformed back into the dilapidated church, and the dying priest from the past became one of the four fake priests beating him. One now had a broken rod embedded into the flesh right below his clavicle.

Zeus blinked and the image shifted.

"Not a rod," Zeus grunted in satisfaction. "The black dagger."

His first blade.

He didn't remember throwing it, but the Blades didn't always need his mind to react, just the use of his body.

Cutting the rope wrapped around his chest, he removed it, as the stunned priests got right with the impending death of their brother.

The plan wasn't to kill, but fuck it, plans changed all the time.

Adjusting the damaged red devil mask, he unbound the rope tangled around his legs, and stood, pulling his black blade from the man's chest as shock transformed into rage in the three remaining men surrounding him.

As one, the men pulled their arms free of their robes and let the upper portion fall to their waists where the robes were bound by rope. They pulled more deadly medieval looking weapons from their robes, flails, ball and chains, weapons to create pain.

Zeus re-sheathed the black blade against his lower back, shed his jacket, detached the Kusarigama from the bullet-proof vest, then shed the vest, his shirt, and shoes before wrapping the Kusarigama's chain around his forearms and fisting the hilts.

Kragen remain seated at the pew, his eyes gleamed as the men encircled Zeus.

The priest with the cudgel was the first to lung. The tip of the scythe-like blade entered the man's neck plunging all the way through to the other side before Zeus pulled, ripping his whole throat out.

The side of Zeus's mouth ticked up as he looked at the remaining two priests, and Kragen.

Zeus's watch vibrated.

Sabrina looked down at her wrist, her heart taking off like a grayhound out the cage.

"Sirius!" she shouted, turning off the living-room lights and flattening against the wall to peek out the front room window.

The lights in the back of the house went dark as well.

"Go below my daughter, you and the child must be safe."

She wished she were that person. Wished she could let others sacrifice themselves to save her, but that wasn't how she was made. She'd always been the one to stand in the chasm, willing to fight, willing to take whatever punishment came, whatever outcome resulted from protecting her mother, protecting her sister.

She didn't know how to be different even for Zeus, even for Bri. They were added to the list of those she'd die to protect.

But surviving, that would forever be a part of her reality until it wasn't.

"It's me and you, old man," she said. "You have your weapons, I have my weapons, we'll be okay."

"Do you see what comes?"

Shit! She forgot. Moving to the laptop on the table, she checked the various areas the camera covered.

"There's only one person; he entered from the side gate, dressed as," she squinted at the screen. "Dressed in monk's robes."

It was like the specter of Cornelius walked the grounds, and one by one the cameras went down.

"Perhaps someone from the convent? Perhaps my son is hurt—"

"Zeus could be half dead and he'd still never send someone here."

"So, we kill," Sirius resolved.

The weight of the situation couldn't erase her sudden smile.

He sounded so much like his damn son it was uncanny.

Had to be something in the bloodline, she thought. These men named after Gods and Stars couldn't deny each other if they wanted.

"We kill only if we have no other choice," she amended.

She wasn't against the police stepping in after the fact. Maybe it would lead to a more far-reaching international investigation into the Consortium.

"Shit," she whispered.

One of the shrubs near the front gate was on fire. The last few years of living in California made her hypersensitive to fires in dry places.

Without hesitation she unlocked the door, hatchet in one hand, and slipped outside, searching the area before sprinting over and kicking dirt and gravel onto the burning plant, making it smolder. Remembering the water pail on the side of the house ran and grabbed it, making sure that no one entered the house through the front door as she emptied what little water remained, ensuring that the burning bush was no longer a fire risk.

A loud crash from the back of the house sent her running through the front door and down the hall, heart racing faster than her feet, fear and guilt threatened if Sirius died because of her decision to have Mama send Carl to Zeus.

Lifting the metal meat mallet off the island as she passed it, she launched at the monk with a bloody gash cut across his chest. She sliced with the hatchet, cutting the bastard across the back, from shoulder to waist. The edge of the blade hit something solid at the monk's hip and sheered away from his flesh. He roared in pain, turned enraged eyes on her, punching her forearm and wrist. The hatchet cluttered against the floor. He backhanded her hard enough to cause her stumble to the left, disoriented. She heard a popping, knew it was a muzzled gun. When she righted herself, she saw Sirius and the robed man struggling for the gun in the monk's hand, aimed towards the ceiling.

Sabrina swung the mallet, striking the back of the monk's thigh as Sirius knocked the gun out of the other man's hand. The gun flew through the open door and landed on the graveled ground.

Sirius lifted his cleaver and would've taken the man's arm off at the elbow if the monk hadn't grabbed Sabrina by the throat and thrown her into Sirius, causing them both to tumble through the door, landing hard on the ground.

The monk peeled off the upper half of his robe and let it fall around his belted waist, reminding Sabrina of the samurais in one of Zeus's old Japanese action-dramas.

Focus Sabrina, she berated herself, scrambling off Sirius, who wasn't moving. Why wasn't Sirius moving?

The monk pulled an arm's length wooden stick from his rope bound waist.

"Where is the child?"

"Not here."

She spat out a wad of bloody saliva as she pushed away from Sirius. His eyes were closed. *Don't be dead, open your eyes*, she willed.

"Lie to me again, bitch, and I'll cut out your bloody tongue."

"I don't understand why you're here, why you're doing this, you're supposed to be a man of God."

"The ways of God and men are not for you to understand woman. We command, and you do as your bid. Where. Is. The. Child?"

"If you're so in with him, you better ask Jesus, because I'll die before I tell you where she is," she said, slipping two throwing knives from their sheaths as she scuttled farther from Sirius and stood.

"Interesting. That's what your dead lover said. But your death is not an issue, you will die. All who played a part in my sister's death will die. As penance. A life for a life. Your life for Delilah's. Zeus's life for Cornelius'."

"Joke's on you, asshole. Cornelius didn't want to return to your little brotherhood. He wanted to be free, even if it was in death."

"The child?"

"Not your business."

"So be it."

She flung one of her throwing blades at him and he

deflected it with his rod. She threw the other and this one scraped the side of his face.

She smiled.

He lunged and she dodged one blow from the rod only to be struck in the chest and knocked on her ass. She scrambled to get up but couldn't get her footing as she concentrated on defending her vulnerable parts against his blows.

Her arms and legs took the brunt of his beating.

He grinned when she arched in pain as a blow landed across her upper back.

The motherfucker was toying with her, taking pleasure in her plain.

A blow glanced off her skull and for a minute the world shifted dizzyingly. She growled in frustration and pain, as she fell back to the ground, resting her head against it as she fought to stay conscious.

She hadn't trained day in, and day out, hadn't wrestled with the demon of Kragen in her dreams, only to lose her life and family so easily.

She covered her head, but the reign of blows to her shoulder and chest said she just might lose despite everything she'd done.

Reaching for her last blade, she felt him crack the rod over her wrist and felt it nearly slip out of her fingers.

Her hand tingled where the blade rested.

To the left.

She could have sworn someone whispered those words, but Sirius was still not moving.

She dragged herself to the left as the monk advanced confidently.

"This has been entertaining," he said, breathing hard. "But the Shepherd wants the child to replace Delilah. It's an honor really, better than she would've received from that useless Kragen. So you see, your struggle has been in vain. There are many who will look after her as she grows."

It was the way he said *look after* that made her stomach roll.

Against all of Zeus's training, she released the blade, followed the voices instruction, and reached to her left.

"Look after this, you son of a bitch," she said, gripping the monk's gun.

She aimed and fired.

The bullet pierced his forehead obliterating his third eye.

The monk's head snapped forward an instant after the bullet snapped it back, and the monk fell like a tree. She moved to avoid being crushed beneath him and stared at the cleaver that split the back of the monk's head.

Looking up, she saw Sirius stumble the wall and slide down it until he sat in a crouch, resting his hands on his bent knees.

"Tres bien," he huffed. "Very good with gun, not so good with knives. You focus on working with guns; blades for you – back up only."

She laughed, then pressed her palms into her skull to manage the pain.

"It's gonna break Zeus's heart, but I agree."

Reaching for the blade that *may* have instructed her, she held it, felt her palm tingle.

"The Blade Spirits protect us in whatever way they deem necessary. But don't tell Zeus about me dropping the hatchet," she pled, as she moved to sit beside Sirius.

"I think, for this, he knows," he said before engulfing her in a bear hug she didn't know she needed. Wrapping her arms around him, she wondered why the hell she was even crying, before determining it had to be Sirius. He gave off strong parent energy, and she hadn't been held with that kind of energy since well before her mother passed.

Though Mama was Mama, her comforting felt wild, feral. The kind that only her Brood – and Carl, could draw solace from.

She looked over at the monk's body.

Was she also crying for the man she killed?

No, more the man she didn't kill in that gold and white room, so many weeks ago.

Putting a bullet through the monk's head seemed to have also vanquished the specter of Kragen, and for the first time since that night, she didn't feel any lingering fear.

Because she'd defended herself and survived.

Because she was loved.

No matter which direction she turned, there were people loving on her, offering friendship, fighting for and with her.

The dead man signified more than killing Kragen, it was letting go of the anger and guilt she felt around not protecting Sam. It was releasing the experiences of wanting love and settling for toxicity, abuse, and the deep loneliness no one could penetrate before Zeus.

She'd woken up on a warehouse floor, lost herself in the silvery gaze of a man who saturated her world in blood.

"We'd better call the police," she said.

"Bon, good plan."

She hoped Zeus's plans were faring as well.

He wouldn't admit it to Sabrina, but there *was* something about returning to the place it all began. Shedding blood in the first place your blood was shed; as Terry would say, symbolically destroying the ones responsible for destroying his innocence.

His Kusarigama sliced through the gut of another of the priests, and he felt the full effect of his lopsided grin as he sliced the ear from another. Moving in close he hacked the hands off another.

This place birthed him into the world, and the Blade Spirts ushed in his re-birthing.

None of these motherfuckers was getting out of here alive.

He was leaving a grisly tableau, but it was only fair. Let everyone see what rotted through the foundation of this place. *Let them all see.*

He growled as he hacked through them, smashed his black dagger through the

eye of one fake priest and jerked the blade before the man slumped to the floor.

His blades sung and danced. The specter of death salivated in the shadows, waiting to collect.

The Shepherd's sacrificial lambs were disciplined, skilled, and could with stand high levels of pain, but they only knew how to serve a shepherd, had no fucking clue about what it meant to go to war with the Blade Spirits.

Something silver streaked past him and he ducked out of the way, turning around when he heard gurgling from behind. A metal projectile was lodged in the throat of the man he'd left unconscious. A semi-automatic fell to the ground.

If he'd left the vest on it would've saved him, but Zeus had removed it, and again the spirits protected him.

"You are pure perfection, brother."

Zeus turned back around to see a shadow separate from the darkness near the wall. Zeus growled, ready to cut the life from the speaker, but the spirits paused his hand. He shook his head, pulling himself fully back into this world; death had never spoken to him in a Nordic accent.

The man who stepped into the candlelight was just that.

A man.

Platinum hair lay against his skull like a newborn's. Black plastic framed glasses surrounded unrepentant black eyes that danced as if death was a joke. His skin was a shade lighter than Zeus's, but golden enough that they could be related.

Zeus attempted to mimic the man's smile. Didn't like the feel of it so his frown returned.

The man was pristine, looked cultured, normal.

Zeus knew a disguise when he saw one.

"Carl?"

Both their gazes swung to the man who had sat frozen on the front pew as his would-be assassins had been cut down. There was hope, and fear, and an attempt to disguise the later, as he addressed the man who stepped towards the front of the church.

"Have you come to save me from this killer?"

"In a manner of speaking Mr. Kragen, yes I have. Is that not so, brother?"

Zeus's gaze flicked back to Carl.

"We're brothers?" His asked, his voice was still rusty as his humanity tried to reassert itself.

It was possible they were related.

Carl laughed gently as he donned black clawed gloves.

"I think we are, yes. Perhaps twins. Yes, I think this might be true. Twins in spirit. One light and one dark. And to be clear brother, I am the dark one." Carl's humor disappeared. "I will take care of things here. My gift to you and our sweet Mama." His eyes... twinkled.

Zeus gazed at Kragen.

The man's demeanor was smug. He'd obviously misread the situation.

Zeus shrugged. Not his problem.

Gathering his clothes and all his weapons into one place, shifted the scalpel into his fist as he moved over to Kragen.

"Guess it's not meant for me to kill you," he said, using the scalpel to superficially slice the flesh along Kragen's collarbone.

Kragen touched the wound, then brought his fingers to his lips, tasting his own blood as he smiled.

He stopped smiling when his arm fell heavily at his side.

Kragen's eyes widened as the paralytic kicked in and he was unable to move.

Terror danced behind his eyes.

"I'd planned to take your head so you and your son would recognize each other in the afterlife." He took all his belongings and walked backwards towards the shadows, as Carl stepped more solidly into the light. "Powers that be planned different. Bri will never know you."

Carl waved pleasantly, his hands now resembled something mixed between Freddy Kruger's and Wolverine's. "So long, brother."

Zeus cast one more look at Carl, before he walked away.

"That motherfucker is weird," Zeus muttered, but waved his hand in a silent goodbye wave.

Walking out of the back of the church, he stepped into the cool night with only the sound of flesh and metal and muffled screams trailing behind.

Returning to the hospital, Zeus cleaned himself, as well as any evidence that he'd been there, before making his way to one final stop before heading home.

CHAPTER TWELVE

The home still smelled of last night's meal, but unlike then, now the space was quiet and emptied but every one of its three inhabitants.

Kneeling beside the bed, Zeus peered down at her, and rested his chin on the mattress' edge, watching as his mother slept through the soft snores from the other side of the bed.

He could see the young girl his father adored in the features of the older woman, but what he couldn't do was understand what he perceived to be a heartless act. To abandon Sirius, to abandon him, yet sleep so peacefully.

He pulled his black blade, wanting her to wear a scar; something to show the world that she had cruelty in her.

"I wondered if you would really come," Zahira said softly, opening her eyes, gazing at him in that sad way he didn't like.

"Why?" he gritted out.

She closed her eyes and he was ready to cut her lids off. Force her to see him.

Tears fell from the ducts and corner of her eyes.

He waited, unmoved.

She opened her eyes and dragged the back of her hand across her face as she sat up.

He rose, stepped back when she swung her legs over the side of the bed and stood in her nightgown. She was as small as Sirius was big.

"Allez," she said, grasping his hand and walking him towards the living room. She released his hand just long enough to pull a heavy trench coat off the coatrack, then walked him to the balcony doors as if he were a child and motioned for him to sit in one of the two wrought iron chairs.

"Sit, please."

He sat, pulled out his phone and took a photo of her, took a photo of the city and then, moving his chair closer to hers, leaned in and took a picture of the two of them. In the silence, he placed the phone on the miniature table next to him, before distancing himself again.

Sabrina and Zuki would need evidence of him having what seemed to be an enjoyable time with Zahira, because he didn't plan on returning.

Reaching into the coat's pocket, Zahira pulled out a pack of cigarettes and lighter, lit up and took a deep drag, looking towards the heavens as she blew the smoke skyward.

Zeus frowned at her.

"Stress release, oui, only for une situation d'urgence," she waved.

"This an emergency situation?"

She smiled; waved the cigarette suspended in the v of her small, fine, manicured fingers.

"I think when my son, who I believed dead, breaks into my house and sits beside my bed with a knife in his hand, then oui, *perhaps* an emergency."

Her eyes held a bit of devilment.

But she wasn't wrong.

"Why?" he asked again.

He had his own family to return to, but with the police at his home, being here served a purpose Mama... Almaya, had said. It felt wrong to call her Mama in the presence of his own mother. Even if–

"Ton père, he was like star, warmth yes, and his presence has... how do you say," she made a fist with her free hand and pulled it towards her in demonstration. "Gravitational pull. Warmth with the power to burn."

She looked ahead at the cityscape.

"Moi, I felt like nothing. And this was intentional, yes, because a nothing half Algerian French girl was easy to control in a country at war with Algeria then. If you control the child, you control the willful woman who would have had no problem returning home to fight and raise her child alone."

"Your father."

Sirius already told him the man was a racist motherfucker.

Zahira nodded.

"He was a retired officer wounded before the War of Liberation. He was obsessed with your grandmére; but obsession is not love my son, it is not healthy."

Zeus thought of Kragen-the-son, and the lives destroyed and lost because of his obsession with Sabrina's sister Samantha.

What kind of father would he have been to Briana? A worse one than his Zahira's father, he thought, blade twisting through his fingers.

"He used you to control your mother."

He knew of France's history, remembered the hundreds of Algerians killed in 1961 before the War of Liberation ended a

year later. He was never allowed to forget who and what
he was.

"Did he hate you or did he love you?"

Her smile was sad as she took another drag on the
cigarette.

"I think a lot of both. When your father came into my
life, he was like the sun when too many of my days were dark
and gray. Ton père, he is like... life. And because he cared for
me, protected me, they stole his freedom away. I told them
and told them, *he protected me, he defended me*, but I think the
boys, my father, those boys' fathers, I think they plan for
this." She cleared her throat. "And then your father was gone.
And weeks later I discovered I was blessed with you."

Her hand patted his knee.

"*You* made me want to fight, to live," she shrugged. "My
father hid me away in the convent. Not even ma mère knew
where I was, but the irony, I was only kilometers from home,
yet if felt like a world away."

She reached for his hand and held it fiercely. "I had you for
days. I was so young, and you father, he was like a God to me,
so his son had to be a God, so I named you Zeus. My lighten-
ing-eyed baby." She was crying again. "I tried to find you, I
went back again and again, demanding to know where my son
had been taken but nothing. I gave up hope. I was was once
again nothing but now I'd lost everything. What was there to
live for?"

She shrugged and waved her sadness away as if all her
words were used up.

"You tried to kill yourself."

"In my mind and spirit, I was already dead. My body just
needed help understanding this. I was in the hospital many
months. And when released, my mother took me, divorced

my father. And except for the one time he came for me and I told him to go fuck himself, I never saw him again."

She'd fought for him. Wanted him. He'd been one of the loved babies he'd spied on in the maternity ward, but they'd stolen her from him.

"You got better?" he asked.

"Oui, as good as a mother can get when she loses half her heart and half her soul."

"Me?"

"You."

The blade stilled and something shifted in his chest, making space.

Zahira stood, bent over him, clasped his face in her hands and kissed both his cheeks, before resting her forehead against his.

"If your father wasn't dead, I'd kill him for you," Zeus told her.

"Such a good son," she laughed. "You were the most beautiful boy. Thank you, thank you for finding me, so I can see you alive, know you are good... dangerous, but good, yes?"

She smiled and sat back down.

"A good man, a good father, you are a blessing."

He swallowed.

The blade spun through his fingers as if given a jolt of electricity.

He had to go home, he had to tell Sabrina everything. Thank her, tolerate her *I* told *you*'s, fuck her into silence, and talk with Zuki.

The loud banging at the front door made his mother jump, but Zeus sat thinking about what movies to watch for tomorrow's movie day with Bri.

Hearing movement from the bedroom, he turned to see

the hall illuminate, and his mother's husband walked out, tightening the belt of his green paisley robe as he rushed to the door.

His mother tossed the cigarette quickly and opened the doors to the balcony staying at his side.

Zeus slipped his blade into its sheath and pulled the hem of his shirt over it, as his grandmother joined Victor at the front door.

Zeus placed his mother slightly behind him as he walked back into the house.

"What is all this?" Nabeela hissed in French. "This is a *respectable* family, why do you come, banging on this door as if a den of thieves lived here?"

The three officers outside the door apologized, but their faces hardened when they saw Zeus stop in the middle of the room.

"Are you Zeus?" One of the officers asked in English.

He nodded once.

"Zeus—"

He was going to say *like the God*, but his mother stepped in front of him protectively.

He looked down at her bemused.

"What is this about?" Nabeela asked.

"His fiancé has been trying to get in touch with him. There's been a death at his home."

"Mon Dieu!" his mother cried out; her hand pressed against her throat.

Zeus growled, took a step forward and the officers took a step back.

"Wait mon amie," Zahira said to Zeus, then looked back towards the cops. "Who is dead?"

His heart thumped like fists beating against a coffin door.

If things went according to plan his family was safe, but Carl had been with him, not at the house. If Sabrina called the police, she was safe.

A death, the officer had said, that meant only Sirius or the intruder.

"A man is dead, killed by your fiancé and your father."

Zeus smiled.

"Where have you been tonight?"

"You see where he is," Victor snapped.

"He's been here getting to know his mother, his family. Until recently we'd all believed him dead," his grandmother said. "But after so many years, Allah brought him home to us."

"Yes, our records show that you were raised at St. Catherine's," he said it as if the convent's name left a nasty taste in his mouth. "Were you there tonight?"

"I was there earlier today with my family, showing them where I came from, then we came here and had dinner. I was home all day until I came to visit with my mother tonight."

"A quelle heure?" The officer asked.

"Nearly three hours ago," his mother said, surprising him.

"Do you mind if we search you, search your vehicle?"

Zeus shrugged and moved towards the door, but Victor held up his hand.

"I will come; if my stepson needs representation, I will be the one providing it."

He left the room to dress.

"Never again will this family be railroaded by the unjust," Nabeela spat out. Zeus lowered his gaze so the cops wouldn't see the laughter in his eyes.

"Come my son, don't forget your phone," his mother said softly pulling him to the balcony where she picked it up from the table and handed it to him.

"I have spoken to your Almaya," she said. "She is good mother, cares for my son when I could not. Unlock phone please."

He did and she breezed back into the house.

"Have you seen my granddaughter, let me show you," she said to the police, flipping through the latest photos on Zeus' phone without a care. Her and Nabeela crooned over the photos, picture after picture, until Victor came back in the room – to the officers' obvious relief.

"Come back tomorrow for lunch," Zahira said.

She must've seen his hesitation.

"Your family is *our* family; they are always welcome." She waved dismissively. "And David's children, they are hysterical pigeons, nothing to be concerned about."

He shrugged, unwilling to commit without Bri and Sabrina being okay with it too.

At the car, the cops, of course, found nothing. One officer sniffed Zeus and he frowned and growled at him.

The office shook his head at his partner.

"There was a fire at St. Catherine's, the remains of six bodies were found. The accelerant used was some kind of jet fuel. There's no way you could've set the fire. It cannot be washed away so easily, non."

"I need to get back to my family."

Victor gripped Zeus's hand and shook it. "We will see you tomorrow. Bring Sirius; I hear he is a chess master, but so am I. Tell him I said he will lose horribly, this will make him come."

Zeus promised to relay the message and left, unconcerned that the police followed at a distance during his drive home.

EPILOGUE

Laying with his left arm draped over Sabrina's pelvis, his head resting just below her breast, caressing her belly as she stroked her fingers though his hair, was his new favorite position.

"That woman is a trip." He could hear the smile in Sabrina's words.

Sabrina had listened to everything he'd told her about what happened in the church, not leaving out any detail. Not even his descent into violence, proving he was worse at interrogating than fucking Bride, and Bride didn't know shit about interrogating.

"Mama's like a fucking hydra," Sabrina continued. "You cut the heads off one of her plans and three more spring up to replace it."

"Yeah... didn't anticipate her calling Zahira and Victor before I even decided to go there. That shit was last minute," Zeus said. "And I definitely didn't see you calling Mama, forcing her to have Carl guard my back. You should get a belly button ring; you have a sexy stomach," he said, dipping his tongue into her navel.

She grunted.

"First of all, we'll see how sexy you find my belly after this baby expands it to the size of a watermelon. Secondly, nobody *forces* Mama to do anything. But my gut told me to send him to you."

"Well, the fake priest came here, which means Shepherd knows of this place. And that possibility is the reason I wanted Carl here."

"I already apologized for that. Profusely."

He smiled. "But I'm thinking that level of disobedience demands shit like unlimited genuflection. And never-ending acts of supplication."

She snorted and bopped his skull with her knuckle.

"You wish."

"I *do* wish," he rose up on his elbow and looked down her stomach. "You see what I mean with the violence, Zuki? Now, go to sleep, so I can punish your mother appropriately."

"Really Zeus, again?"

"A-fucking-gain," he confirmed, slipping his hand between her legs and stroked until her moans and startled gasps shifted into undulating hips that moved in their own rhythm of need, as if he hadn't shown her twice before the leisurely pace he wanted to set for tonight.

He liked this pregnancy thing.

One stroke, one kiss, one suck, and she was gushing.

Slipping his head between her thighs, he did a deep dive into her sex and didn't resurface until her hands scrambled for the pillow beneath her head and pressed it against her face, screaming her release into it.

Zeus crept up her body and rose to his knees, guiding the

tip of his erection into her glistening entrance as she flung the pillow to the side.

"Now, apologize."

"Fuck you," she said lethargically. "I'm not apologizing again."

He shrugged, angled her knees high and wide and slammed into her until his dick was so deep it had nowhere else to go.

They'd all had a trying evening, he wanted the dance to be easy tonight, but she couldn't just do what he asked. He really didn't ask for much.

"I need to hear your sincerity when you say it this time," he told her.

He gave her a chance, rolled his hips as he eased into her, waiting for her words.

"You know what, do what you need to do, because you've gotten your last apology from me tonight." Her brow arched. "Did you hear the sincerity in that?"

Humph.

Okay, he nodded, cracked and rolled his neck, then gripped and kneaded her ass cheeks.

"I'll show you what I hear," he said, thrusting slowly, listening to the almost imperceptible glide of him moving in and out of her. He heard her soft sighs, her whimpers as he leaned forward, and kissed her breasts, licked them, tongued them, sucked them.

"You hear me?" he asked.

This was the pace he wanted, but he'd move at the one that she deserved.

He lowered himself on top of her, pressed his lips against hers.

They kissed violently.

He adjusted her knee over his shoulder and pumped harder, faster, making her ass jiggle as his middle finger chased her clit in fast circles, making her sob, making her forget to reach for the pillow as she begged.

"I hear it," he nodded as she came, he fucked her incoherent apologies, made of words not worth the letters used to form them, from her lips.

He lost himself in mindless fucking, working her hard, fast.

His sack tightened, his dick vibrated pleasure, and the force of his ejaculation blew a hole through him, shattered him, and her body captured the pieces, held them together until he lowered himself on to her body. He watched her intently as she dozed.

She was beautiful, she just was, and she was violent and emotional and strong, yet she still chose him.

Shifting his weight to the side, he butted his nose again the ear.

"It was a good idea ya know, to find my family." He closed his eyes, resting his head against the side of her neck. "Thank you."

She scrambled to sit up. "I *told* you! I knew it would be worth it, I knew you needed this. Next time just listen to me and–"

He covered her mouth with his hand and dragged her back down to the bed, wrapping around her until she stopped struggling, and gave up the need to gloat.

"Thank you for trusting me," she said, lacing her finger through his. "You keep trusting me and I keep loving you more. Love you, Big Man."

"Starting to think people can't help but to love me. I guess I'm that guy."

"You're an idiot."

"Your idiot."

She laughed softly. "Always."

When Sabrina woke to an empty bedroom, explosions, crashing cars, screeching tires, and gun shots blasted on the other side of the door.

Movie day had started without her.

There was no telling what the three of them were in there watching, but she doubted it was appropriate for an almost eight-year-old.

Rising from the bed, she slipped on a t-shirt and stood, waiting for a wave of nausea that never came.

"Poor Zuki, your daddy tired you out too, huh?"

If high doses of sex kept the morning sickness at bay, they were going to need to change mattresses every month.

Walking to the bathroom, she brushed her teeth and showered before stepping back into the bedroom to dress in a pair of black cotton pants and its matching off-the-shoulder top that exposed her mid-drift.

Instead of joining the family in the living-room, she went back to the bathroom and pulled fresh linen from the closet and walked it back to the bed for Zeus to make up later.

Feeling benevolent she even stripped the soiled linen and placed them in the laundry.

"Look at you, being all domestic and shit," she told herself. "See Zuki, by the time you get here, I'll have it all together."

As much as she enjoyed being a paramedic, she didn't want to return to that work. She definitely didn't want to go back to working in an office.

For the first time in her life, she didn't have to work to survive; she could choose what direction she wanted to go, and part of that choice was being a mother, and the other choice was to go back to school to become a medical examiner.

Her gaze returned to the disheveled bed and she smiled smugly.

She would never have to apologize again after this, she thought, once she was done making the bed.

"Greatest apology ever," she said, before marching into the living-room, turning off the television, and standing in front of it, unbothered by the boos and popcorn being thrown at her.

Pulling a cheese flavored kernel from her hair and shook her head at Sirius.

"Et tu."

He smiled angelically and shrugged.

She rolled her eyes and ate the popcorn, then pulled Zeus off the couch and dragged him towards the bedroom, Briana and Sirius following closely behind.

Shoving Zeus inside the room she waved magnanimously.

Zeus's silvery gaze moved from her to the bed, and back to her.

"I finally made the bed!" she pointed out, because they all seemed to be a bit slow this morning.

Zeus leaned over and dragged his hand over the top blanket, then yanked it completely off.

She shrieked in rage as he continued to strip the rest of the bed.

"If the nuns saw this you would've been beaten to within an inch of your life. And you would have deserved it," he muttered low, as if she wasn't in the fucking room.

"That was really, really bad," Bri whispered to Sirius.

Sabrina swung around, feeling truly hurt and betrayed.

"Is it your eyes, mon fille?" Sirius asked with concern. "Was vision damaged by hit on head last night?"

Zeus scoffed.

She was ready to curse all of them out, but she took a deep breath and calmed her nerves because they weren't going to make her feel bad.

"Wow... just wow."

She left the room and went to make her something to eat when even Zuki started rebelling against her.

"Here grab the ends," she heard Zeus say in the bedroom.

"What did the bed do to deserve that?" Briana asked, as if she were truly confused.

"I think, maybe doctor come and check her out, oui, to be safe? I call." Sirius said.

Sabrina chewed on a slice of ginger, went to the table out in the back yard and ate her food in peace. She didn't have to listen to them disrespecting her

"Come," Zeus said, watching her from the doorway. She turned her back and continued to eat.

He walked outside picked her up out of the chair and walked her back into the house, depositing her on the bedroom floor in front of the newly made bed.

She begrudgingly admitted to herself that her bedmaking skills had a lot to be desired.

Briana handed Zeus a pillow and Zeus directed Sabrina to the head of the bed.

"You will only be allowed to fluff pillows and place them against the headboard."

"Oh, I guarantee you, I'm not even doing that."

"Woman's brain," Zeus looked knowingly to his father.

"Place the pillow there and we'll never speak of you making the bed again," he promised Sabrina.

She snatched the pillow and a small black velvet pouch with a drawstring flew from the pillowcase and landed on the bed. She frowned, picked it up, and looked at Zeus, who shrugged and frowned.

It was the way Bri danced from one foot to the other, that made Sabrina's heart race.

It was the proud smile on Sirius face.

Slowly opening the pouch, she poured the contents into her palm

Two shiny titanium bands with a black inlay at the center bordered by gold twinkled at her.

Inside the band, black cursive letters spelled out *Zeus's woman.* Zeus reached out and placed the smaller one on her finger.

The inscription on the larger ring read *Sabrina's God Zeus*

"Zeus made them," Bri said. "I found them last night. By *accident*," she said with wide eyes. She'd been snooping.

"Marseille or Paris?" Zeus asked.

Yes, her fantasy of marrying in France was their other reason they were here.

She twisted the ring around her finger.

"What's wrong?"

"I thought the getting married in France would be the most romantic thing in the world, but..." she thought of the Brood, of her best friend Randy and Mrs. Jace. "I just want to celebrate this with our family back home."

She turned to Sirius, but he spoke before she could ask.

"I go where my son goes."

"We'll get married in the forest," Zeus said.

Oh *hell* no.

"I promise you, I will not be getting married in that haunted forest around your cabin."

His eyes laughed at her. "I meant at Mama's House."

Oh. Okay. That was kind of perfect. For them.

She wrapped her arms around his waist and kissed him.

"I understand now," he said, pressing his forehead against hers. "Why I was left to guard you in that warehouse. It was because I had to learn there was more, that I was more, and you were there to make me see. Love wasn't possible before you Sabrina Samora. Now it's all around us. I love."

And she felt his love, felt his words, felt him like one feels the sun, like a desert feels the rain, like the dark feels the light. Reverently and completely.

ACKNOWLEDGMENTS

A loud and proud thank you to all the readers who continue to support and encourage me DESPITE the strain I put on your patience. I've said it before, and I'll say it again: You all are awesome and I'm grateful for your support.

Special thanks to:
Editor: Ali Williams @ aliwilliams.org
Cover Artist: Carolee Samuda @ Creative Design Concepts
http://creativedesigns2.com
You helped make the words and the images right and I'm grateful.

To my Ride and Lives (because we're not ready for the whole dying thing yet), you all are amazing and have helped shape this book and my commitment to the profession of being an author:
As always Lady D and Marsha McNairy you, your feedback, and support are invaluable.
To my No Name Beta (lol) you have been an ardent supporter since book one and I thank you for being willing to squee with me over this book.
Marisha Goodman and Tia Stewart when I think of amazing women, accountability partners, sharing hearts, *Talented*

creatives/writers, and author friends, I think of you. Thank you for being willing to hold space that allows us to be us.

Love you, Shay

ABOUT THE AUTHOR

Shay Rucker loves to write stories that mashup elements of love, fantasy, action, and horror. Her debut novel, On The Edge of Love, was the 2016 Swirl Awards winner for Romantic Suspense. When she is not writing, Shay is balancing her main working gigs, friends and family, and plotting new international adventures.

Join Shay's newsletter at http://eepurl.com/dkteVT to receive the latest!

ALSO BY SHAY RUCKER

Mama's Brood Series

On The Edge of Love, Book One

Unleashing the Storm, Book Two

Paranormal Romance:

The Kilgarin's Gift

Printed in Great Britain
by Amazon

MAMA'S HOUSE

When a man is named after a god, it only stands to reason that he shows deference to nothing but the Blade Spirits he's bound to, and no one, but the woman who's bound him in her love.

When that same man assumes the responsibility of a child whose survival requires that he adapt, he must move towards a level of existence he's never aspired to.
So he learns things, like considering other people's feelings; smiling... trying to mean it; corralling his darker urges so that his new family can know a happiness he was never allowed.

But a life of domestication doesn't ensure the safety of his expanding family. Not when soulless men want to take what he's fought for, shed blood for, and is willing to die for again and again.

In this latest edition of Mama's Brood, Zeus and Sabrina return to Zeus's beginnings, facing old demons and new enemies while fighting to hold on to a love they never believed existed for people like them. Will they finally get their happy-ever-after? Or will they discover that their moments of happiness are not meant to last a lifetime?

MAMA'S BROOD 3

ISBN 9780997473391

9 780997 473391

90000